FAULT IN THE STRUCTURE

Gladys Maude Winifred Mitchell – or 'The Great Gladys' as Philip Larkin called her – was born in 1901, in Cowley in Oxfordshire. She graduated in history from University College London and in 1921 began her long career as a teacher. She studied the works of Sigmund Freud and attributed her interest in witchcraft to the influence of her friend, the detective novelist Helen Simpson.

Her first novel, *Speedy Death*, was published in 1929 and introduced readers to Beatrice Adela Lestrange Bradley, the heroine of a further sixty six crime novels. She wrote at least one novel a year throughout her career and was an early member of the Detection Club, alongside Agatha Christie, G.K Chesterton and Dorothy Sayers. In 1961 she retired from teaching and, from her home in Dorset, continued to write, receiving the Crime Writers' Association Silver Dagger in 1976. Gladys Mitchell died in 1983.

ALSO BY GLADYS MITCHELL

Speedy Death
The Mystery of a Butcher's Shop
The Longer Bodies
The Saltmarsh Murders
Death and the Opera
The Devil at Saxon Wall
Dead Men's Morris
Come Away, Death
St Peter's Finger
Printer's Error
Hangman's Curfew
When Last I Died
Laurels Are Poison
The Worsted Viper
Sunset Over Soho
My Father Sleeps
The Rising of the Moon
Here Comes a Chopper
Death and the Maiden
Tom Brown's Body
Groaning Spinney
The Devil's Elbow
The Echoing Strangers
Merlin's Furlong
Watson's Choice
Faintley Speaking
Twelve Horses and the Hangman's Noose
The Twenty-Third Man
Spotted Hemlock
The Man Who Grew Tomatoes
Say It With Flowers
The Nodding Canaries
My Bones Will Keep
Adders on the Heath
Death of the Delft Blue
Pageant of a Murder
The Croaking Raven
Skeleton Island
Three Quick and Five Dead
Dance to Your Daddy
Gory Dew
Lament for Leto
A Hearse on May-Day
The Murder of Busy Lizzie
Winking at the Brim
A Javelin for Jonah
Convent on Styx
Late, Late in the Evening
Noonday and Night
Fault in the Structure
Wraiths and Changelings
Mingled With Venom
The Mudflats of the Dead
Nest of Vipers
Uncoffin'd Clay
The Whispering Knights
Lovers, Make Moan
The Death-Cap Dancers
The Death of a Burrowing Mole
Here Lies Gloria Mundy
Cold, Lone and Still
The Greenstone Griffins
The Crozier Pharaohs
No Winding-Sheet

VINTAGE MURDER MYSTERIES

With the sign of a human skull upon its back and a melancholy shriek emitted when disturbed, the Death's Head Hawkmoth has for centuries been a bringer of doom and an omen of death - which is why we chose it as the emblem for our Vintage Murder Mysteries.

Some say that its appearance in King George III's bedchamber pushed him into madness. Others believe that should its wings extinguish a candle by night, those nearby will be cursed with blindness. Indeed its very name, *Acherontia atropos*, delves into the most sinister realms of Greek mythology: Acheron, the River of Pain in the underworld, and Atropos, the Fate charged with severing the thread of life.

The perfect companion, then, for our Vintage Murder Mysteries sleuths, for whom sinister occurrences are never far away and murder is always just around the corner …

GLADYS MITCHELL

Fault in the Structure

VINTAGE BOOKS
London

Published by Vintage 2014

2 4 6 8 10 9 7 5 3 1

First published in Great Britain by Michael Joseph Ltd in 1977

Vintage
Random House, 20 Vauxhall Bridge Road,
London SW1V 2SA

www.vintage-books.co.uk

Addresses for companies within The Random House Group Limited can be found at: www.randomhouse.co.uk/offices.htm

The Random House Group Limited Reg. No. 954009

A CIP catalogue record for this book is available from the British Library

ISBN 9780099584056

The Random House Group Limited supports The Forest Stewardship Council® (FSC®), the leading international forest-certification organisation. Our books carrying the FSC label are printed on FSC®-certified paper. FSC is the only forest-certification scheme supported by the leading environmental organisations, including Greenpeace. Our paper procurement policy can be found at www.randomhouse.co.uk/environment

Printed and bound in Great Britain by Clays Ltd, St Ives plc

CHAPTER 1

Hardened in error by pride of intellect

Osbert Swineborn proposed to Dora Ellen at the New Year's Eve dance which his mother, who knew Dora Ellen to be the only child and heiress of a wealthy expatriate American, had given for that purpose.

'Well,' said the young lady, 'well, all right, O.K. then, but a condition goes with it and, until that condition has been fulfilled, I want no part in your future life and happiness.'

Osbert had no inkling of what was coming. However, grateful for his mother's efforts on his behalf and mindful, as ever (for he was a dutiful son) of her wishes, he promised that he would do anything – positively *anything* – which would result in his winning Dora Ellen's hand in marriage.

It was not that he loved the young woman. The ability to love was not one of his endowments. It was simply that he agreed with his mother, who had often, although without rancour, expressed the opinion that he was unlikely ever to make what she called 'a decent living' for himself and that therefore his aim should be to marry a wife whose dowry would result in his leading that life of ease and leisure for which both his mother and he were convinced he was best fitted.

'So what do you want me to do?' he asked his fiancée. 'Just say the word and, if I can, I'll do it.'

'That's binding on you, then. Look, honey, it's this way. I am not going through the rest of my life calling myself Dora Ellen Swineborn. I'm kind of allergic to hogs.'

'Oh, dear!' said Osbert. 'Is that really the case?'

'Yes, *sir,* that's really the case, so what's wrong with planting that cute little letter *e* some place else and changing that little letter *o* into a little letter *u*?'

'Such as how?' asked Osbert, who was no dabbler in poetry, although he had heard of Shakespeare and had enjoyed Miss Joyce Grenfell's rendering of an imaginary American mother attempting to introduce an imaginary American child to the glorious works of Percy Bysshe Shelley.

'Such as spelling it Swinburne, of course,' said Dora Ellen impatiently. So, by deed poll, accustomed from his earliest years to female domination, Osbert slightly but significantly changed his surname and Dora Ellen became Mrs Osbert Swinburne.

When, in due course, her son was born, the mother insisted that he be named Alfriston (after his place of birth) and Calliope, after the Muse of epic poetry. With a name like A. C. Swinburne, she contended, a poet of some kind he was surely destined to become.

'Alfriston Calliope?' said Osbert doubtfully. 'A bit tough on the poor little so-and-so, isn't it? Besides, I thought Calliope was a kind of steam-engine.'

'Honey, don't show your ignorance,' said his wife.

'Anyway the kid will only be called Alf if you stick to this Alfriston label, and I've always thought Alf was, well, you know, rather a common sort of name; the sort of name they give barrow boys and plumbers' mates and the chaps who wear cloth caps and belong to Unions.'

'Alf?' said his wife distastefully. 'There was Alfred the Great and Alfred, Lord Tennyson. I never heard either of them referred to as Alf.'

'He might even be called Al, like Al Capone,' said the father rebelliously.

'Whatever he's called, he will be able to sign himself A. C. Swinburne,' retorted Dora. 'I would have liked to name him Algernon Charles, but I guess it would hardly do to plagiarise that far. Anyway, so far as what he's to be called is concerned, we must insist on Alfrist, nothing shorter.'

'Alfrist?' said Osbert. 'Oh, yes, Alfrist would be all right, I suppose. Rather classy in a way. Alfrist C. Swinburne? Yes, your father might like that! It sounds quite American, I mean to say, doesn't it? It may reconcile the old buster to our marriage, what?'

'We never *would* have married if I hadn't seen the possibilities of this A. C. Swinburne set-up,' said Dora Ellen, at last uncovering what had always been a mystery to her spouse, for Osbert knew that, in spite of his mother's favourable opinion of him, he was anything but an eligible *parti*. 'Pop acted kind of tough when I broke the news,' Dora Ellen went on, 'and if I hadn't of gotten this Swinburne idea I guess I would have listened to his arguments.'

'But who *was* Swinburne?' asked Osbert. He had wished to ask before, but had lacked the courage. His wife looked at him with pity and contempt.

'All I can say, honey,' she remarked, 'is that I guess I'm aiming to see that Alfrist gets a better education than you appear to have gotten for yourself.'

'I was too delicate to be sent to school,' said Osbert. 'I was educated at home.'

'I wonder what *that* explains?' said Dora Ellen, handing the baby to the nurse. 'The first thing you do, honey, you put his name down for a dozen or two of these Eton and Harrow schools. That way we'll be sure he gets in somewhere good when he's old enough. A boy with the name of A. C. Swinburne has got to be going places.'

What would have happened to A. C. Swinburne had his mother lived became a matter for speculation, for she died when the child was thirteen and in his first term at his public school. After her death, Osbert discovered, to his dismay, that she had had but a life interest in her fortune and that her father, who had returned to America, had married for the second time and now had a son of his own. He had diverted his fortune to this child of his old age, leaving Alfrist with a small annuity payable when he attained his majority. Nothing whatever was willed to Osbert, who, for the first time in his life, was faced with the hideous prospect of having to earn a living for himself and his son.

The boy was taken away from his expensive public school and sent to a State school where he did well enough so far as work was concerned, but where he was never popular and soon became known as 'teacher's creep'.

That was by no means the worst of it. At his public school a waggish master had referred to him as Algernon Charles, to the mystification of the form. They were more familiar with Latin than with English verse. Questioned on the matter by his peers, Alfrist, who had no intention of disclosing the truly dreadful names bestowed on him by his American mother, had replied that he supposed the master had been trying to show what a funny swine he could be. As the master in question was known and despised for his untimely and unkind wit, this definition of his humour was accepted.

Unfortunately for Alfrist, his new comrades at the State school discovered, from the classroom anthology of English poetry which was supplied by a paternal government, exactly what the public school master had had in mind, although they knew nothing of the incident. Someone found that the book of poems included Swinburne's *Itylus,* so the lad was set upon in the playground one dinner-time and, to joyous yells of 'Swallow, my sister, O sister swallow', a cake of soap from the washroom was forced chokingly into his mouth.

From that time on, Alfrist set himself two objectives: to change his name as soon as he could (but not, for he was an intelligent although hardly a likeable lad, until after he had made sure of the annuity he was to be given by his American grandfather) and to fit himself to take vengeance upon society. He reached neither of these goals while he was still at school, but kept them in the forefront of his mind against the time when he should attain his majority.

Having reached his sixteenth birthday and his O levels, he received, to his surprise and chagrin, the now very unwelcome news that his father proposed to take him away from school and put him to the task of beginning to make his own way in the world and pay for his keep.

'But I can't,' he said blankly. 'Not yet. I've got my A levels to do.'

'I don't earn enough to go on keeping both of us,' said his father. This was at the end of the Easter term and for another three mon*hs Osbert allowed the subject to drop. He had no wish to try conclusions with his son too soon. The long summer holiday at the end of the following term would be a better time to elaborate his point of view, he thought.

He himself had tried one kind of unskilled employment after another, disliking each a little more than the last. He particularly objected to his present job although it brought in a little more money than any of the others he had tried. The work necessitated the wearing of overalls and sometimes breaking the nails of his so far fastidiously-kept hands. It also brought back unwelcome memories of his autocratic wife who, as time went on, had become more and more authoritative and exacting and (what in his opinion was worse) more and more inclined to hang on tightly to the purse-strings.

One of the economies on which she had insisted was that small adjustments, tunings and running repairs to the family car should be made cheaply at home instead of expensively at a garage. Osbert had attempted to rebel against this, but his bid for independence was soon quashed. In the course of the years, therefore, he had become a reasonably competent mechanic and when the time came for a show-down between himself and his son, he was in the employment of a garage proprietor who specialised in tarting up and reconditioning used cars and selling them at a reasonable profit.

One of the perquisites of this particular employment was that there were opportunities for the mechanic to go joy-riding in the repaired cars. When he did so he imagined himself to be the owner and the car a brand-new and expensive model. During the school holidays, he occasionally took Alfrist with him on these jaunts, but there was little fellow-feeling between them. Alfrist despised his father and when it became clear at the beginning of the summer vacation that, instead of joining the privileged Sixth Form to sit his A levels, he really *was* to be put out to work, he renewed his protests.

'I want to go to University,' he said. 'You've only got to keep me another two years, father. I'll get a student grant after that. Why can't I stay on?'

'Money. Do you realise what your clothes cost, let alone your food?'

'Mr Churt says I'm a cert for my A levels. I got nine Os, father.'

'Yes, I know you did and they ought to stand you in good stead. You could get a very decent job in a bank, I shouldn't wonder. You wouldn't want your poor old dad to go on keeping you for another five or six years, would you? Even with a grant you'd cost me a lot of money.'

'I'm your son and I reckon it's your job to see me through. Look, dad, I'm not a cretin. I get jolly good marks all the time at school. I'm worth being given my chance.'

'If your mother had lived, everything would have been different, you see,' said Osbert, with the resentment he always felt when he thought about his wife.

'Well, she didn't live, so now it's up to you,' said the youth realising, however, that he was fighting a losing battle.

'I can't manage it, son. My health isn't good. Never has been. It's time you took on some responsibility. What would you do if I pegged out as, with my heart condition and the sort of work I do, I easily might?'

This argument carried no weight with his unsentimental son, who treated it with the contempt he felt it deserved by saying:

'Oh, if anything happened to you, I should go and live with my grandfather in America, I suppose.'

The school term ended in mid-July and, as had been the case for several years, Alfrist found himself at a loose end with six or seven weeks of summer holiday to get through as best he might. He had no friends with whom to spend his time. He was still only tolerated at school, not liked. There were no holiday outings for him, either, except an occasional drive with his father when Osbert was trying out one of the reconditioned cars.

He might have found himself temporary employment, as many of the other lads did, but he felt that this would be playing into his father's hands. He also decided that the kind of job he could get was far beneath his notice, for, with his mother's obstinacy and pertinacity, he had inherited her wealthy-woman's snobbishness. In the hotels in a neighbouring seaside town there were vacancies for temporary waiters, kitchen hands and porters, but Alfrist did not think for a moment of applying for any of them.

The consequence was that he was restless and bored. He spent a certain amount of his time in the reading and reference rooms of the local public library, but also, less admirably, he became adept at shoplifting, first because he wanted sweets or fruit which he had no money to buy; then just for the thrill of seeing what he could get away with and still escape detection. Later, because he found that in the Saturday street-market it was possible to dispose of stolen goods without being asked too many questions about how he had come into possession of them, he became more daring, but knew he was living dangerously.

Sometimes he really did think of writing to his American grandfather; sometimes he thought of his father's question: *What would you do if I pegged out?* Sometimes he thought of both at the same time. On the last Wednesday of the holiday, when they were out for one of their infrequent spins in a recently reconditioned car, he made his last appeal to Osbert.

'You do mean to let me go back to school and take my A levels, don't you, father?'

'Sorry, old man. Shouldn't really have let you idle away these last six weeks,' said Osbert. 'You might have been settled in a nice little billet by now. Pity it didn't occur to me sooner. I'm so much accustomed to your long school holidays that I never thought of putting you to work. Well, you've had your fun, so the best thing now is for you to turn up at school the first day of term and ask your headmaster for a reference. That's another thing I've only just remembered. We ought to have seen to it before you left.'

'If I go back they'll expect me to stay, so why jolly well can't I?' demanded the boy.

'There's no question of it, son. I've told you that I simply can't afford to keep you on at school any longer. I'm surprised you don't want to pull your weight to keep our home going. It's not a very manly attitude, is it?'

'I'd be able to pull a much heavier weight if I got my A levels and my degree,' said Alfrist sullenly.

'That's enough! We'd better be getting back to the garage now,' said Osbert. 'I've got a customer coming to look over this car at six.'

'When you've turned her, let me drive a little, Dad. You know I can handle a car,' said Alfrist, changing his sullen tone to one of conciliation and pleading.

'Public road. You're under age,' objected his father.

'There's never much traffic along here. Anyway, couldn't we go back by way of the fenced lane? That's always empty and there are never any police about.'

'We can go that way if you like,' said his father, relieved by the change of tone, 'and, if there's nobody about, I don't see why you shouldn't drive for a bit.'

The fenced lane was approached by a straight, unfenced road across a stretch of common, and the 'fencing' (so called) was a high stone wall bordering a large estate on the left-hand side of the road. At one time the road had been gated and the evidence for this remained in the form of two stone pillars between which the gate had been hung.

Alfrist took the driver's seat after his father had made certain that the road was clear and they approached the stone pillars at a speed which Osbert, himself a cautious driver, thought was excessive, as, just beyond the pillars, the little road dipped sharply and bent away to the right.

The danger was upon them before either the driver or the passenger was aware of it. Up the rise came a car travelling fast in the opposite direction. Alfrist, racing towards the gap, pulled sharply over to avoid a collision, but misjudged the width of his vehicle and crashed it into the stone pillar at the left-hand side of the way. He himself escaped with shock, bruises and a severe shaking-up. Osbert, in the passenger seat, was killed.

After the inquest the wife of the garage proprietor took Alfrist back with her and gave him a cooked meal. She was a large-hearted Lancashire woman and had conferred with her husband over what was to happen to the boy. They offered him a job as petrol-pump attendant. He would live in, learn how to repair and refurbish used cars and eventually take on the work his father had done.

It was not a bad offer to a boy of whom they knew nothing except that he was the son of a shiftless and lazy sire who, like

Tom Sawyer, could work when he had a mind to, but was precious seldom in this happy and useful state. However, they made the offer and were disconcerted and surprised when Alfrist thanked them and said loftily that he would think it over and let them know his decision.

When school re-opened after the end of the vacation he went along to see his careers master, only to find that he had never been taken off the school roll and had been assigned a place in the Lower Sixth form and was to begin studying for his A levels.

'You said nothing last term about leaving, did you, Swinburne?' the master enquired.

'No, sir. I was hoping to persuade my father to let me stay on. I thought he would have written a letter if he really intended to take me away.'

'He intended you to leave?'

'He said so, sir. He wanted me to get a job – get something to allow me to earn, sir – but I don't know what I could do. I came along to see whether you had anything to suggest, sir.'

'It seems a pity not to stay on and take your A levels.'

'I have to keep myself, sir. I haven't any money.'

This was not quite true. His market dealings in stolen goods had left him with enough to pay the rent and keep him in food for a week or two.

'No relatives who could help you?'

'I've a grandfather in America, sir, but I've never met him.'

'I think we must get in touch with him.'

Dora Ellen's father was a man who had never approved of his daughter's marriage, but he was not insensible of his obligations to her now completely orphaned son. He made a settlement on the boy to tide him over until he came into the annuity already promised to him when he came of age and felt that this provision relieved him from further responsibility.

Meanwhile, as these satisfactory arrangements were still being concluded, the chairman of the school governors had taken an interest in the (as he thought) unfortunate youth. He took him to live in his house until other provision could be made for him. Sir Anthony was neither a clever man nor an astute reader of character, but he was given to good works and trusted all men until he found them out, which he was both loth and slow to do.

His charitable activities brought him into contact with a great many people. He also possessed, together with a trusting nature, a considerable bump of curiosity and it seemed to him strange that his young ward should have no relatives living except for an American grandfather. He ferreted around and eventually dug out a distant cousin of the boy's father, a man with whom Osbert had never had any contact. This man, high up in academic circles, was persuaded to regard himself as a long-lost uncle to Alfrist. He was a childless widower whose wife had died in a car accident, so he felt sympathy for the bereaved youth. Old Sir Anthony retained interest in him and the young man did both his guardians credit in some ways although, unfortunately, not in all. His distant relative, now styled his uncle, was a distinguished but not a wealthy man, so that, while in his care, Alfrist was suitably clad and fed, but was not provided (in his own opinion) with sufficient pocket-money for his adolescent needs, neither was he given the motor-cycle for which, in spite of the accident which had resulted in his father's death, he yearned, nor the fashionable gear he wished to wear.

However, he obtained his A levels and the offer of a place at no fewer than three universities. His so-called uncle might have been prepared to take the boy into his own ancient and distinguished university, where he was Warden of one of the Colleges, but a couple of years of acquaintanceship with Alfrist had convinced him that neither his own interests nor those of the young man would best be served by this. Alfrist was impatient of control and readily agreed that it would be better for him to accept a place in another university rather than to be continually under the eye of his uncle, even though he did not express his opinion in exactly those words.

During his first year in College Alfrist contracted debts. In spite of his American annuity, his student grant and a small allowance from his uncle, he never had enough money for what he saw as his needs. His uncle settled the debts, but with such ill grace that Alfrist spent the long vacation with old Sir Anthony, who still looked upon him with an indulgent eye.

Judging that the time was ripe, Alfrist confided to the old man a desire to visit his American grandfather. Sir Anthony, always sentimentally inclined, advanced him the money for his fare and sent him off with his blessing. Alfrist went to Paris on the money, enjoyed himself in various slightly dubious ways and returned with a story that his American grandfather had refused to see him, but that the annuity would still be paid.

To strengthen his position with Sir Anthony, Alfrist spent the rest of the vacation tutoring a backward boy for Common Entrance. There was nothing wrong with his own brains and he proved a capable and conscientious mentor. This was not entirely to his credit for, as usual, keeping one eye upon the main chance, he thought that the boy might be useful to him in the future. He was the son of a wealthy industrialist and Alfrist decided that if university life did not suit him, there might be plums awaiting him in the industrial world if he played his cards wisely with regard to his tutoring of the rich man's lad.

His immediate future, as he saw it, involved the obtaining of a respectable degree and then a university post. After that, Fate, which had been kind to him on the whole, would be certain, he thought, to put opportunities in his way. He had no intention of living on a lecturer's salary for the rest of his life, but it would do to begin with while he looked around for better – i.e. more lucrative – employment.

After he left college Alfrist obtained a post at a northern university and soon found himself back in an atmosphere to which his schooldays had accustomed him. His fellow-lecturers either barely tolerated him or actually disliked him, for he proved to be arrogant, self-opinionated and conceited. However, so far as his uncle and old Sir Anthony knew, he kept out of trouble. At the age of twenty-six he published a novel which was kindly noticed but did not sell and, two years later, a collection of poems whose slightly erotic flavour brought him a certain amount of notoriety, if not exactly fame.

He had published his poems under the name of Theddeus E. Lawrence, hoping, by this means, to attract the American market, and it was as T. E. Lawrence that he decided in future to be known, thus accomplishing a schoolboy resolve. The hoodwinked old Sir Anthony was delighted with him and showed his good opinion by suggesting him as co-trustee with a nephew of his (Sir Anthony's) own, for a minor who was to inherit a fortune; the same boy, in fact, as the one whom Alfrist had tutored and who had now entered his seventeenth year and had been left an orphan.

It seemed to Lawrence, *né* Swinburne, that the accident to his own father had been the most fortunate of occurrences. Death, he realised, was, among other things, a solver of problems. But for his father's demise, and the manner of it, he would never have been taken up by Sir Anthony. He cultivated the old gentleman and had high hopes of becoming his heir.

CHAPTER 2

Those who are wise in their own conceit

The garden seemed hardly the right setting for the conversation which was taking place in it. Its tranquillity and its age-old peacefulness were at odds with the matter which was being discussed. Its smooth green lawn was bordered by a broad, moss-grown path and between the path and that part of the old city wall which formed a bastion between the college and a busy street there were flower-beds in their summer colours of red, yellow, white, blue, purple, cream and pink. Trees and shrubs made a background to all this variety of tints and hues and, as though to add a touch of romance to the scene, there was a long flight of stone steps which led up from a scent-filled rose-bed to the top of the crenellated wall. It served as a reminder, perhaps, of old, unhappy, far-off things and battles long ago, but it was overgrown with lichen now, and never used.

Dividing the lawn into two unequal parts was the famous lime walk. Between its two rows of trees whose pale flowers hung in clusters, filling the air with their elusive fragrance, the two men strolled up and down.

Beyond the lime walk a retaining dry-stone wall separated the lawn from the terrace and from another riotous pageant of summer flowers; this second mass of colour was thrown into masterly assertiveness by the long façade of the fifteenth-century College buildings which acted as its background and its foil.

This long line of pointed gables which made up the west front of the College was broken in the middle by a bold and massive tower which formed part of the Warden's lodging, and it was the Warden himself who was pacing up and down between the rows of lime trees with his guest, the pair so much engrossed in their conversation that the garden, as such, went unnoticed and, so far as one of them was concerned, brightness fell from the air and no birds sang.

'So there it is,' he said at last. 'Old Sir Anthony will have to be told, I suppose, and what we are to do if a scandal of magnitude is to be avoided, I cannot think. I suppose you have no suggestion to offer?'

If some arrangement could be made – if somebody, for instance, was willing to guarantee the sum involved – could Lawrence pay back the money by instalments?'

'I know of nobody who would be prepared to offer such security. My own fortune falls short of forty thousand pounds by a considerable margin and in any case I would not be willing to reduce my sister and her daughter to penury on Lawrence's account. He does not deserve it. It is not, either, as though he were my son. He is not even, strictly speaking, my nephew.'

'He is not in the hands of the police?'

'It is only a matter of time, and a short time at that. I have managed to persuade the auditors to keep their findings to themselves for a few days, but they were very unwilling to allow us even that much grace.'

'Does Lawrence say why he had such need of the money?'

'He tells me nothing except to deny the charge in its entirety.'

'Has he ever been in trouble before?'

'Not in trouble of this magnitude, and not since his undergraduate days. At that time there were occasional debts to be settled and two or three jilted shopgirls had to be compensated. Fortunately he had seen to it that he was not a student here, and as Warden of Wayneflete I was not at all anxious to have him bring his profligate habits to this University, let alone to my own College, so we were in agreement so far as that was concerned.'

'Is it possible that he is being blackmailed? You say you have settled debts for him before, so one assumes that he would have mentioned the fact if it was simply that he owed the money to someone – although, to a young man on a fixed salary plus, as I understand it, a small annuity, forty thousand pounds must seem a pretty considerable sum, even in these days.'

'Considerable enough for him to know I could not replace it,' said the Warden grimly.

'I wonder whether you would like me to have a word with him?' suggested Sir Ferdinand Lestrange.

'I was hoping that you would offer to do so. Your legal training may enable you to elicit something from him which he has not confided to me. I feel that if only we knew why he needed the money so badly, there might still be some way of helping him cope with this dreadful situation. He is staying in College for the present. You will find him in the Senior Commonroom.'

'From which I excused myself after dinner, as you had suggested this talk. I will return there.'

The Senior Commonroom, like the west front of the College buildings, belonged to another century. It was part of the Tudor wing and its principal features were the linenfold panelling of its walls, a magnificent fireplace and a ceiling heavily plastered with meaningless arabesques and with oval lozenges incorporating the coats of arms of the various benefactors to the College.

Surprisingly, the College bore the name of the founder of Magdalen College, Oxford. Above the fireplace were carved the mitre and the arms of Bishop William Wayneflete and on the ceiling in the largest of the ovals were 'in lozengy ermine and sable a chief sable with three lilies therein' the chaste ecclesiastical bearings of the late fifteenth-century prelate, one-time headmaster of Winchester College and, later, the Provost of Eton before he became exalted to the See of Winchester.

In front of the fireplace stood Lestrange's quarry. Thaddeus Edison Lawrence, as Swinburne now called himself, was a tall, thin man of thirty-two. His untidy, dark hair was worn collar-length, and he had large hands which he was using freely to emphasise his remarks to his only companion, an elderly, totally deaf don named Bagg. Lawrence had a peevish, sensual, melancholy face which reminded himself of Lord Byron and others of a disgruntled although rather handsome camel.

As soon as he saw Lestrange enter the room he broke off what he was saying, raised his eyebrows and stared distastefully at the intruder. Lestrange, however, ignored him and joined the Dean and the Bursar, who had been arguing a point of law and who seized upon Lestrange to give a verdict.

Finding that the mountain was in no hurry to come to Mahomet, Lawrence strolled over to the group of three, listened to the argument without joining in it, and then said to Lestrange, 'I saw you walking in the garden with my uncle.' His voice was not cordial.

'Yes.' The College dignitaries moved away, so, for the moment, the two men were alone. 'I should be glad of a word with you.'

Lawrence led the way to the rooms which had been allotted to him during his stay in College. Here he sported his oak and then produced whisky.

'Sit down,' he said ungraciously, 'and if you intend to question me, please make the catechism short.'

'Very well, I'll be brief to the point of brutality. I suppose you're being blackmailed,' said Lestrange.

The other was so surprised that he almost dropped the decanter.

'Why on earth should you suppose that?' he demanded.

'It seems obvious, my poor chap. Look, Lawrence, come clean and I'll see what I can do to help you. I owe that much to your uncle.'

'Nobody can help me. I'm supposed to have embezzled forty thousand pounds and haven't one chance in ten million of being able to prove that I did nothing of the sort. The auditors think they know better.'

'Forty thousand is not such a vast sum. Relax and tell me the whole story. It *is* blackmail, isn't it?'

'Yes, but not for forty thousand pounds. That is ridiculous,' said Lawrence, after a pause.

'You didn't think of telling the blackmailer to go to hell and to spill the beans and be damned?'

'I couldn't.' He hesitated and then resumed: 'It's a matter of a previous marriage. It would kill my wife if she knew. You see, I thought Coralie was dead when I married Margaret, but a few months ago she bobbed up again and is bleeding me of sums I can hardly afford in return for not exposing me.'

'But if you had reason to think she was dead, you have a good case. I call to mind R. v. Tolson, where an almost similar set of circumstances arose. In that case, a woman named Martha Ann Tolson had good reason to believe, on the evidence of his elder brother, that her husband, a sailor in the merchant navy, had been lost at sea on a voyage to America. Some years after his presumed death she re-married, supposing herself to be a widow.

'However, her first husband turned up again and her second marriage was held to be bigamous. As she was able to plead that she genuinely believed the sailor to be dead, she was not convicted. There was no *mens rea*, you see.'

'What does that mean in law?'

'In layman's language it means that Martha Ann Tolson had not meant to commit a criminal act; in other words, when the act was committed it was committed in good faith. She had not a guilty mind. It seems to me that, if you truly believed your wife was dead when you married Margaret, you have a good defence and can have no reason to give in to blackmail.'

'But Margaret would know that I had been married before I met her.'

'Did you not tell her?'

'No. I was not even divorced, you see.'

'What steps did you take to make certain that your first wife was dead?'

'Well, she wasn't dead, was she?'

'How long were you married to her before you parted?' asked Lestrange, without commenting upon this equivocal answer.

'Two years. I've been married to Margaret for seven, but there was an interval, of course.'

'So it was how long since you had seen or spoken to your first wife?'

'Nearly twelve years. I went north to take up an appointment when I left College and did not take her with me. She was hardly an asset in university circles. She is a chorus girl.'

'Nearly twelve years? I suppose you are certain it *was* your first wife who turned up again?'

'Oh, yes, I insisted on a second meeting to make sure, although I hadn't any doubt the first time. We arranged to meet in a pub out on the Bicester road where I thought there was little chance of running into anybody I knew.'

'And you recognised her again?'

'Oh, yes, there was no doubt it was Coralie. I was in my second year at university when I married her, but she hadn't changed a bit. She made herself very charming in her uneducated, low-class way and said she was down on her luck and asked me what I was prepared to do about it.'

'How long did you live with her?'

'I've never lived with her. I had rooms in College when I married her, and I could hardly take her there.'

'So the marriage was never consummated.'

'Oh, yes, it was. We used to meet secretly at her mother's place when she wasn't on tour.'

'But you said you'd never lived with her.'

'Oh, I see what you mean. I thought you referred to our setting up an establishment. We never did.'

'Was there a child?'

'I don't know. After I'd done a bit of private coaching I got this job at a northern university and after a time – I forget how long – Coralie and I ceased to correspond. It began with me. I stopped answering her letters. All she did was ask for money. I sent her what I could, but she kept on pestering to join me. By that time I knew what a fool I'd been to marry her. We had nothing whatever in common and the tone of her letters became vulgar and abusive in the extreme.'

'She never attempted to seek you out and challenge you face to face to acknowledge her as your wife?'

'It was soon obvious that such was not her aim. All she wanted was money and for a time I was glad enough to send it so long as she kept away from me. Then I changed my digs without leaving a forwarding address. I was living out of my College – all the staff and students up there do – and in my next letter I did not give her my new address. I kept my eyes open after that, thinking that she would put in an appearance and renew her demands, but she didn't, and very soon I thought I had found out why. A friend, an undergraduate who was in my confidence, wrote to me and told me to go back at the first opportunity and study the grave-stones in the town cemetery.

'I realised what he was telling me, so on my next vacation I went back. I searched among the graves until I found the one I was looking for, the grave of Coralie St Malo.'

'She wasn't using your name, then?'

'She'd stuck to her stage name. She'd been a chorus girl, as I said, and I expect she thought St Malo sounded better than Lawrence. At any rate, there the grave was, and mighty relieved I was to see it. Meanwhile I'd fallen in love with Margaret and, as I thought, I was free to marry her. My uncle was pleased with the match. Margaret is a junior don at Abbesses College, in this his own University, so he knew her. Naturally he knew nothing of Coralie. At least I'd had the sense to keep her dark.'

'So you assumed that the happy ending was in sight when you married for the second time.'

'Wouldn't anyone? And then, clean out of the blue, I ran into Coralie in the town market here at the beginning of the Long Vacation. I had the shock of my life, I can assure you. I must simply have stood and gazed at her. She said, "Well, dearie, have you come back to keep me in the style to which I am not accustomed? I know all about your second marriage, you rat." I managed to gargle out something to the effect that I thought she was dead and that I'd seen her grave. She laughed in a very nasty way. "That was my poor mum's grave," she said. "Her stage name was the same as mine. Ever been had, you two-timing Casanova? Well, you've done for yourself now, haven't you? I suppose you're prepared to pay me to keep my trap shut? Wouldn't do you *or* the lady don much good to be labelled as bloody bigamists, would it? All right, my greatest lover of all time, I want my first instalment and I want it soon." '

'And you met her again at the pub on the Bicester road?'

'Yes, I hoped I could persuade her to call off her vendetta. However, as I said, she made herself very pleasant at first, but she stuck to this outrageous demand for what she was pleased to call alimony, although there had never been any question of divorce. She mentioned her marriage lines and said that they were in a safe place, but that she could and would produce them at any moment if I refused to pay up. I was scared out of my wits because I knew she meant what she said, so, in despair, I gave in. You see, she could prove that when I married Margaret it really was bigamy. Well, all that was bad enough and now, on top of it, comes this charge of embezzlement. It's untrue, but I simply don't know how to refute it.'

'All right, Lawrence. For the sake of your uncle and his position in this my old College, I am prepared to guarantee you a long-term loan of forty thousand pounds, which will clear your name for the time being. I shall then go into the matter with your auditors. Who are they, by the way?'

'Lestrange, Collins and Dobbs.'

'My cousin Harry? Well, that's a bit of luck for you, anyway. Once the money is repaid, I can fix Harry and ask for his discretion, so that nothing need be made public. That isn't for your sake, but for Sir Anthony's and the Warden's. A stink of this nature wouldn't do either of them any good. I shall need you to sign an undertaking to repay the money, of course, and with reasonable interest.'

'There's been some mistake, some ghastly mistake, Lestrange. I'm going to get another firm of auditors on the job.'

'You would be very unwise to do that. I have influence with Harry, but none with any other firm if you have a second audit carried out.'

'Oh, well, if you can get your cousin to stall for a bit, I suppose that will help. I'm going on holiday the week after next with old Sir Anthony, so I shan't be on hand for a bit.'

'Yes, it might be as well to get him out of the way while we settle things up and put you in the clear.'

'And I suppose you expect me to thank you into the bargain!'

'Oh, hardly! I feel I know you better than that,' said Sir Ferdinand, going towards the door.

CHAPTER 3

A place of security in times of insecurity

The Stone House just outside the village of Wandles Parva on the edge of the New Forest belonged wholly to the eighteenth century. All the rooms in it were spacious, high-ceilinged and airy. The most pleasant room of all, thought Sir Ferdinand, meeting his mother, Dame Beatrice Lestrange Bradley, at the conclusion of his visit to Wayneflete College, was the drawing-room.

It had two doorways, one leading in from the hall, the other to an ante-room. Both doors were augmented by six plain panels: two, small and square, at the top of the door, four, rectangular and beautifully proportioned, below. Both doorways were topped by broken pediments evolved from an earlier style, that of Renaissance architecture.

In the drawing-room, as in every room in the house with the exception of the kitchen and the servants' quarters, there were bookcases. These were low and long and placed on either side of the elegant fireplace in the drawing-room, taller and more sombre in the dining-room, and lining all the available wall-space in the library.

The bedrooms were stocked with lighter matter; poetry, essays, humorous literature and novels for the most part. In the small study where Laura Gavin, Dame Beatrice's secretary and close friend, carried out such duties as answering letters and typing from Dame Beatrice's manuscripts, the books were on law and forensic medicine; and here, too, were volumes for general reference, encyclopaedias, atlases, motoring and yachting manuals, guide books, year books, dictionaries both English and foreign.

Ferdinand was being given tea in the drawing-room and he had turned the conversation on to his recent visit to Wayneflete College. Having greeted him and announced that she did not care for tea, Laura Gavin, the secretary, had slipped away and left the mother and son together.

'So did you guarantee the forty thousand pounds?' Dame Beatrice enquired, at the end of her son's narration.

'No, mother,' Sir Ferdinand replied. 'A most unexpected thing has happened. Perhaps I should say that two unexpected things have happened. All that I've told you so far is, so to speak, stale news, so I'll come to the reason for my being here. I need your advice.'

'Intriguing.'

'My profession has aggravated and extended what has always been a suspicious mind. However, my cousin Harry suffers no such disadvantage, so I want to know whether you think, when I come to enumerate them, that his unusual suspicions are justified; if you decide that they are, I'd like to know what you think I ought to do about them. Harry is neither doctor nor lawyer, but he has a great fund of commonsense.'

'More and more intriguing! Would you take it amiss if I ventured upon a little wild guesswork?'

'I know something about your kind of guesswork. It's usually founded upon a brilliant series of deductions. Please go ahead.'

'I can scarcely bear to wait for the full details which I trust you are about to supply, but my suggestion is that, since you have not needed to guarantee a replacement of the forty thousand pounds of embezzled money, old Sir Anthony must either have paid the debt out of his own pocket, or else he has died and the money has been repaid out of his estate. That is if I am correct in assuming that Mr Lawrence managed to become so much *persona grata* to the old gentleman as to be nominated as his heir.'

'You must be *clairvoyante*, mother.'

'That is not so flattering an observation as your previous attempt. It is true, then? Sir Anthony is dead?'

'True as true can be.'

'So what is the advice I have to give?'

'Well, everything turns upon this suspicious mind to which I make claim and which gives me cause to think that Harry may be right, although I fail to see what anybody can do about it. The facts are these: a fortune, which was to come to this minor for whom Sir Anthony's cousin and Lawrence himself were trustees, was left for the youth to enjoy at such time as he should come of age. No actual year was mentioned in the Will. I have seen a copy of the testator's intentions and the words *at such time as he shall come of age* are plainly given. Well, of course, when the Will was made, the recognised date for a minor to come of age, unless otherwise stated, was on his or her twenty-first birthday.'

'Ah, yes, I see. A comparatively recent change in the law could have made a difference of three years to the heir presumptive.'

'Exactly. It is now recognised that youths and young women come of age at eighteen instead of at twenty-one. Old Sir Anthony's cousin, the other trustee, had told Lawrence, it seems, that the testator expected his heir to inherit at the age of twenty-one, but the heir himself, not unnaturally, wanted the letter of the law to be observed, and confidently expected to come into his money as soon as he celebrated his eighteenth birthday. There was a legal wrangle and, owing to the wording of the Will, the trustees lost their appeal, although there is no doubt in my mind that their contention was right and that the testator had been thinking in terms of his son's twenty-first birthday and not his eighteenth.'

'If Lawrence was able to embezzle forty thousand pounds, the fortune must be a considerable one.'

'Yes, indeed. Well, the youth claimed his legal rights, the auditors were called in and that is how Harry came to be mixed up in the business, for it was his firm which did the audit. Well, I don't need to stress the result of the auditor's findings. Instead of having three more years in which to make good the deficit or, as I think, make his arrangements to leave the country, Lawrence found himself in a most equivocal position.'

'But what is Harry's problem?'

'Frankly, mother, Harry believes that old Sir Anthony was murdered.'

'Evidence? Has Harry anything to go on?'

'That's the devil of it. So far, there doesn't seem to be any evidence he could offer. The death certificate was quite in order and Sir Anthony was duly buried, the chief mourner being his snuffling heir, Thaddeus E. Lawrence. There we stick. Harry wants me to carry the matter further, but how can I?'

'What was the supposed cause of death?'

'An unsuspected aneurysm blew up while he and Lawrence were on holiday.'

'Unsuspected?'

'Yes. The doctor later declared that, like so many of the wretched things, it was probably congenital, and that Sir Anthony either didn't know of it or had never mentioned the possibility.'

'What about the symptoms?'

'He complained to Lawrence of not feeling well, but, until the symptoms of brain haemorrhage, prefaced by severe headache and vomiting, followed by a coma, appeared, no doctor was informed. By that time it was too late to do anything for the poor old boy and he died in an hour or two without coming out of the coma.'

'So why does Harry think he was murdered?'

'Chiefly because his death was such a fortunate thing for Lawrence; also because he thinks anybody else would have sent for a doctor as soon as the old man complained of feeling unwell. As it was, Lawrence decided to bring him home, and he died upon arrival. Has Harry any kind of a case, medically speaking? So far as I am concerned, although I agree with him over the matter, in law he has none.'

'A mere motive for murder has never been sufficient to prove guilt, as you would be the first to admit. If the medical certificate is in order I cannot see that Harry's suspicions can have any real justification. To show that they are justified he would need to prove that Sir Anthony had called for medical attention when he first complained of feeling ill, and that this had been denied him. Even then one would be faced with the most extreme difficulty in proving criminal negligence, I fear.'

'That's what I've been at some pains to point out to Harry.

The doubt in my own mind is whether there was any need for the aneurysm to have carried Sir Anthony off at all. Of course, he himself could not be questioned. By the time the doctor arrived, the patient was unconscious and died in coma, as I said. *Is* there anything which would look like a burst aneurysm but which would, in effect, be murder?'

'Not to my knowledge and, in any case, a doctor who has issued a death certificate is not to be divorced at all easily from his findings. Who else was in the holiday lodging at the time?'

'Nobody who would have reason for concern about the old man's health. Sir Anthony and Lawrence had rented rooms in a small hotel on the Norfolk coast where they appear to have done no more than take short walks. They did not patronise the public lounge or the television room and no doctor saw Sir Anthony until he arrived home and was already comatose. Lawrence's story is that as soon as Sir Anthony complained of feeling ill he bundled him into a car and took him home so that his own doctor could attend him. He says he telephoned the doctor, who came at once. He says he had no idea that the old man was at the point of death, or he would have called a doctor earlier, in spite of Sir Anthony's protests.'

'In spite of Sir Anthony's protests?'

'That is Lawrence's story and there is nobody to challenge it unless you can think of some way in which Harry can take the thing further.'

'Did Sir Anthony know of the embezzlement?'

'Lawrence says not. He declares that he said nothing to Sir Anthony about it in order to spare him distress for as long as possible. Harry thinks differently. He contends that Lawrence sprang the bad news on the old man while they were on holiday, hoping that the shock would kill him.'

'I doubt very much whether any such contention would hold water, although, medically speaking, it is sound enough. It does indicate, though, if it is true, that the presence of the aneurysm was known to Lawrence. That would be a very serious matter, but one which would be difficult to prove.'

'That is what I told Harry. It seems to me that all we could prove is certain negligence in that there was too much delay in calling for medical advice. Still, if Lawrence called a doctor as soon as he got the old man home – a thing which, no doubt, *can* be proved – I don't think any jury would convict, even if the thing got as far as a trial, and I don't believe it would. The strongest part of Harry's argument is that Lawrence knew he was Sir Anthony's heir and was in trouble over the embezzlement. Against that, though, is the fact (known not only to Lawrence and myself, but to the Warden of Wayneflete) that I had offered to guarantee the money *before* Sir Anthony died.'

'Yes, it hardly seems necessary that Sir Anthony should have been murdered, does it? I think Harry had better forget the whole matter and reflect upon the saying that the Devil looks after his own.'

'I'm sure you are right. Harry went to the length of having a word with the doctor, but only got a flea in his ear.'

'As he might have expected.'

'Yes. Well, now, mother, to other matters, although they are still concerned with Lawrence's affairs. I want to trace this Coralie St Malo woman. I'd like to make quite sure that *she* isn't dead, too. We can't get Lawrence for Sir Anthony's death, but if anything has happened to Lawrence's first wife I think we might have a case. If only to satisfy Harry I'd like to look into things, for I believe, with him, that Lawrence is a thorough-going scoundrel.'

'It has yet to be proved that Coralie St Malo was blackmailing Lawrence.'

'That need not be his only reason for disposing of her. I'd tackle the job of ferreting around for her myself, but I'm tied up with R. versus Verinder at present and haven't a spare moment after today, so I wish you would deputise for me. Will you?'

'I had much rather not involve myself. These things are much better left to the police. Besides, ferreting around, as you call it, is not one of the things I do best, particularly when there is so very little to go on.'

'Not all that little, you know, mother. If there's nothing fishy going on, why do I have such a suspicious mind about Lawrence and his messy little machinations?'

'I cannot tell you. I did not form your mind. I left that to your father and to your mentors and preceptors. But why are you so suspicious? Is there something you have not mentioned?'

'Yes, there is. The University town, as you probably know, has two cemeteries. I have combed both of them to find the Coralie St Malo grave but could not locate it, so I applied in both cemeteries to the persons in charge. They had no record of a burial of anybody called Coralie St Malo and suggested that I might try the various churchyards.

'I thought it possible that Coralie's mother had been buried with full ecclesiastical honours, so to speak, so I did as I was advised, interviewed vicars, pastors and sextons, so on and so forth, but failed to find any trace of any Coralie St Malo's grave, neither was I introduced to Lawrence's helpful undergraduate friend. Oh, well, if you won't involve yourself you won't and I don't blame you, but I *know* Lawrence is a wrong 'un – and I don't just mean the embezzlement.'

In spite of her objections, Dame Beatrice found that she could not avoid involvement. Fate, as she expressed it later, sent to her from Abbesses College a card inviting herself and Laura to the principal's annual garden-party.

The official card of invitation was accompanied by a letter. Part of it ran:

> Do come if you can. We shall be overflown, not with a honey-bag, as Bottom feared Cobweb might be, but with a bevy of reverend signiors (pronounced *Seniors*) and younger married dons with dreadful wives and frightful children, because everybody interesting dashed off on holiday the minute term ended. I know this is anything but an inducement to you to come, but I should be so delighted to see you and the lively Laura again.

'The gardens at Abbesses should be at their best,' said Dame Beatrice, when Laura had read the letter. 'Shall we go?'

'I see that we are invited to stay to dinner and for the night,' said Laura. 'That means evening kit as well as our garden-party get-up. I suppose I shall have to wear a garden-party hat! Ah, well! "One must suffer to be beautiful!" One thing, we need not take George. I can drive and that will do away with any bother about where to lodge him for the night. The end of next week? That will give me time to get my hair fixed and iron my finery.'

CHAPTER 4

. . .a world that changes to a crazy tempo
On the off-beat from the rhythm of eternity

Abbesses College was set in the midst of water meadows on the outskirts of the town and, as its name implies, had been built as a convent for nuns. As was the custom with mediaeval abbeys, it had been built round a cloister and this still remained although it was not much frequented, since it was both dark and damp.

The dampness was due to an imperfectly repaired roof; the darkness was accentuated by the undisciplined tangles of climbing and rambler roses which a former principal of the College had planted in the cloister garth just outside the embrasures which served as windows. The growth of the roses had gone unchecked during the war, when gardeners were hard to come by, and pruning had received little attention since.

What had been the nuns' chapel was now the parish church. It formed the north wall of the cloister, but there was no longer any connecting door between the two. This had been blocked up so that visitors to the church had no direct communication with the College. Of the other original features which remained, the nuns' frater, was now the College dining-hall and the convent kitchen which adjoined it, although it had been completely modernised, still fulfilled its original purpose. The nuns' infirmary had become the College chapel and the abbess's lodging, a commodious building because it had been designed to accommodate important visitors to the abbey as well as housing the abbess herself, had become the house of the High Mistress, as the principal was proudly entitled. Part of the lodging had been made into the Senior Commonroom, but the Fellows, the dons, the students and the servants were domiciled in a large new block which had been erected on what had at one time been the nuns' orchard.

The High Mistress's garden, known as Nuns' Enclosure, was her personal property in that the only means of admittance to it was from the Lodging itself or by way of a small gate to which she alone held the key.

The much larger Fellows' garden was adjacent to it, but the two were separated by a broad walk between two high stone walls, each smothered in free-blooming, climbing roses. There was a doorway in each wall, but only the High Mistress held the keys to both doors, so that she had access to the Fellows' garden, but they had none to hers.

Beyond the gardens the original outer court of the convent was now tree-lined and had flower-beds. It was known as Bessie's Quad after the intrepid Abbess Elizabeth Smallfield, who had held Henry VIII's commissioners at bay outside the gate-house (which was still standing and which formed the main entrance to the College) for three days before she would allow them inside.

Beside the gate-house, but a few yards from it, the nuns' store-house and barn had been turned into garages (lock-ups) for staff cars and a bicycle shed for the students, who were not allowed, for lack of space, to keep their cars in College. Between the bicycle shed and the gate-house was the porter's lodge. It was nothing but a small, stone-built hut consisting of one room and a wash-room. There were two porters who worked four-hour shifts. The gates were locked at night and opened at eight in the morning. This arrangement was occasionally inconvenient, but in the main it worked smoothly. Each Fellow and don had a key to the little, roundheaded door in the huge gate-house portal, but for students the hours of ingress and egress were strictly enforced, and to bring a don in her dressing-gown and slippers to let one in after hours was not a practice worth cultivating.

Dame Beatrice and Laura lunched on the way down and arrived at the gatehouse at three. The enormous gates were wide open, so Laura drove in and was stopped by a uniformed man on duty.

'Police at a garden-party?' said Laura, who, on the strength of possessing a husband who was an Assistant Commissioner at New Scotland Yard, treated policemen with aunt-like familiarity. 'How come, Sergeant?'

'We have to search your car for bombs, madam.'

'What! Has there been a scare?'

'No, madam, but this is a big do. The Vice-Chancellor is expected and the local M.P., besides other celebrities.'

Laura and Dame Beatrice emerged from the car and Laura handed over the keys. The suitcases were taken out and examined and the interior of the car scrutinised before they were allowed to drive on to that part of Bessie's Quad which had been reserved as a parking-lot for visitors' cars.

The gate which ordinarily shut off the walled path between Nuns' Enclosure and the Fellows' garden was open and so were the gates which ordinarily kept the two gardens private from one another. Dame Beatrice, who had visited the College on many previous occasions, led the way into Nuns' enclosure where, as she had expected, the High Mistress of the College was circulating among her guests and greeting new arrivals.

The garden was completely walled in, the buildings which were now the principal's Lodging forming the fourth wall. Below the walls were flower-beds and the centre-piece at the house end of the garden was a well. It had a high stone surround and a fine canopy of wrought-iron work from the top of which depended a bucket and chain, the bucket held below the top of the stone-work so that its utilitarian purpose did not offend the eye. Adjacent to the well were two ancient apple-trees, but they gave little shade and the day was hot.

Laura, whose Highland blood had no sympathy with a temperature in the eighties, noted that over the wall she could see the branches of a magnificent cedar tree; so, leaving her employer (who heeded the heat no more than a lizard on a sun-baked wall) in earnest and apparently entertaining conversation with a group who had come up to renew acquaintance with her, Laura wandered out through the gate, crossed the broad path and entered the Fellows' garden.

Here there was not only the spreading cedar whose shade she

sought, but a bonus in the form of little tables at which tea, cakes, ice-cream and strawberries and cream were being served. The waitresses consisted of one or two maids reinforced by half a dozen women students who were remaining in College for a week or so to take advantage of the facilities offered by the College and the University libraries because they wanted to put in some extra work before going down.

Laura seated herself in a deck-chair, and was soon approached by a student wearing a backless sun-suit, enormous dark-glasses and open-toed sandals.

'Gracious!' said Laura. 'You look more comfortable than I feel!' She removed her festive and detested hat and, grateful for the shade of the cedar which made the hat unnecessary, she hung the redundant lid on a projection at the back of her deck chair.

'We agreed to do our waitress act so long as we could dress as we liked,' said the student. 'The Bursar thought it was all right so long as we didn't turn out in bra and panties or in bikinis. The trouble is to keep old Doctor Giddie at bay. Giddie by name and giddy by nature is that old goat. What would you like? It's all free.'

Laura laughed and opted for iced lemonade. When the girl brought it she was accompanied by another who carried a tray laden with cakes and strawberries.

'I say,' said this second girl, who was somewhat more decorously clad than her companion in that her frock, although backless, was almost knee-length, albeit her feet were bare, 'didn't I see you come in with Dame Beatrice? Do you know her?'

'I am her dogsbody. I type, drive the car, chase away unwelcome visitors, answer letters, look up references, bark, balance lumps of sugar on my nose, jump through hoops at the word of command and sometimes join Dame B in pastoral dances by the lee light of the moon,' Laura replied.

'Could you ask if I can consult her after Hall tonight?'

'Consult her? She's here as a visitor,' said Laura, becoming serious.

'Oh, I know, but, you see, I need a psychiatrist and I can't afford the fare to London as well as paying her fee.'

'Oh, you plan to be a cash customer? What's the trouble?'

'I've been seeing the College ghost, a monk dragging a sack. I need help and – well – is it true that she charges according to one's means?'

'A foolish practice for which I have often upbraided her. All the same, if you want a psychiatrist, well, she's no longer in regular practice, you know. Even if you did attend her London clinic, you wouldn't get her. You'd get one of the three doctors who now run it. She visits every now and again, but that's all.'

'I see.' The two girls left her table, for a stream of visitors suddenly cascaded into the Fellows' garden, so Laura finished her cake, lemonade and strawberries and relinquished her seat in the shade to a plump, blonde woman who was feeling the effects of the sun. Then she wandered around the grounds. She discovered the cool silence of the cloister and noticed that on the side opposite the church an open archway led into a pleasantly secluded little garden and that this, again, opened on to the main quadrangle and the enclosure formed by the twentieth-century College annexe.

An archway between two blocks led to an acreage of grass which Laura deduced must be part of the College playing fields and she was delighted and surprised to see that one boundary of this area was formed by a backwater of the river. She wandered down to it. As it could be crossed by a wooden bridge which had no gate at either end, she assumed that the land on the other side was also College property.

There was a boathouse on her side of the water. Laura studied the stream, noted that it was clear of weed and, as there were dressing-boxes alongside the boat-house, she realised that she was looking at the College bathing-place.

'Lucky devils!' thought Laura. She tried the first of the cubicles. It was open. In two minutes, naked as a mermaid, she was in the water.

Four tables were set for dinner in Hall that evening. Dame

Beatrice sat at the high table with the High Mistress and the more distinguished of the guests, two tables below the dais accommodated the remainder of the invited, and at the end of the long room sat an unusually muted gathering at a table to themselves, the students who were staying up.

Laura found herself seated between two of the reverend signiors referred to by the High Mistress in her letter. One of them asked her whether her husband was a member of the University.

'No, he's a policeman,' Laura replied.

'Ah, yes, I remember. I knew the name meant something to me. Assistant Commissioner Robert Gavin, isn't it? I think I met him once. Tell me, does he still believe in ghosts?'

'I don't know that he ever did.'

'This place is haunted, you know. Oh, yes, it's a fact.' He chuckled. 'It's a scandal, too. The ghost is that of a monk, and the monks were not necessarily or even usually, in early monastic times, ordained priests. I conclude, therefore, that he had no right to visit a convent.'

Laura, who disliked what she called 'sniggery little men,' said calmly, 'The custom of ordaining monks to be priests was begun I believe, by the Augustinian canons who founded houses in England from towards the end of the eleventh century, but the Benedictines and even the Cluniacs, who followed the Benedictine rule but with considerably greater austerity, were slow to follow suit.'

'I see that you have studied your subject,' said her partner, slightly taken aback. 'Anyway, to revert to the frivolous topic of the ghost, you will admit that he had no business in a convent of nuns.'

'Oh, he had *business* all right,' said Laura's other neighbour whom she knew, from the place-names at table, to be the apparently notorious Doctor Giddie.

'I believe he's been seen quite recently,' said Laura. 'One of the students who is staying up claims to have seen him.'

'Where?'

'She didn't say. Incidentally, as I said, I don't think my husband has ever believed in ghosts. I wonder what made you think he did?'

'All Scotsmen, if they're Highlanders, believe in ghosts,' said the don.

Someone opposite contested this and the argument turned on to kelpies, water-horses and the Loch Ness monster, a conversation in which Laura, who was well informed on all these matters, was able to distinguish herself.

'Are you a Catholic?' her partner enquired when, coffee having been served, the guests were standing around waiting to bid their hostess goodnight before departing to their homes.

'No. Why? Oh, you mean because of monasteries. I've always been interested in monastic life and not so very long ago I helped Dame Beatrice to investigate a murder which took place in the grounds of a convent.'

'Oh, I see. Does Dame Beatrice believe in ghosts? You see, I'm a member of a local society for psychical research and we'd very much like to investigate the story of the monk who haunts this College, but, so far, the High Mistress won't give permission.'

'Not even during the Long Vacation when the last of the students has gone down and the College is empty?'

'No, because there is still a skeleton staff of maids in residence. She says they would be so much alarmed by an investigation that they would leave. And in these days, when it's so difficult to get good, reliable domestic help, she cannot take the risk. I thought perhaps Dame Beatrice might persuade her. The ghost of the monk is well authenticated.'

'She wouldn't persuade anybody to risk losing servants,' said Laura. They passed out of Hall and the don took his leave and went out through the Fellows' garden. This was now bespangled with fairy lights hanging from the apple trees and placed around the coping of the well. All were of a sinister shade of blue.

Laura shivered. It seemed to her that the summer night struck suddenly chill. She thought of blue-papered, blue-brocaded rooms in haunted houses. An owl screeched. The trees rustled and talked.

'All the trimmings!' muttered Laura anxiously.

CHAPTER 5

And they go silently away
Saying nothing for fear of betrayal

'Well, what of the day?' said Dame Beatrice when Laura, in dressing-gown and slippers, came to say goodnight. 'I had the impression that at the sight of the Vice-Chancellor you fled.'

'It wasn't the Vice-Chancellor. It was the heat. I spotted a cedar tree on the other side of the wall and made a bee-line for its grateful shade – rather a nice example of transferred epithet, that. It was I who was grateful, and *was* I! What is more, I was waited upon by nymphs and regaled with some of the best 'real' lemonade I've ever tasted, cakes direct from the College kitchen and, although I was not fed with apricocks and dewberries, with purple grapes, green figs and mulberries, I did get a plate of the finest English strawberries together with as much fresh cream as even I could eat.'

'After which you vanished from the scene, only to reappear at dinner.'

'I had no intention of being rude or unsociable, but, except for you, whom one couldn't get near because of the crush, I didn't know a soul and I couldn't imagine that a soul would wish to know me, so I went exploring around and about and had a swim.'

'You are always so enterprising. How did you manage that?'

'I found Parsonesses' Pleasure, or whatever it's called in these parts. It's a bathing-place in a backwater of the river, clear of weed and perfectly lovely. You know – lush banks on either side, with meadowsweet, dog-daisies, tall grasses, purple loosestrife, water forget-me-not and monkey flower.'

'Monkey flower?'

'You're certain to have seen it. Once a foreigner, now naturalised. Biggish, deep-yellow flowers with red spots and a long lower lip to the corona, Latin name *Mimulus guttatus*. Well, I enjoyed myself no end. I swam a goodish way upstream and found that there is a wire mesh across the water to bar boating strangers, I suppose, from witnessing Beauty bathing by a spring. I swam about a mile the other way, too, and encountered a similar barrier. There's a boathouse by the dressing-sheds, so I suppose the girls have about two miles of river-water all to themselves for swimming and rowing. I didn't appear again at the garden-party because I had to get my hair dry and fixed before I could meet the company at dinner.'

'But how did you get *yourself* dry?'

'The sun did most of it and I finished up on the enormous pocket-handkerchief I keep in my handbag in case a tourniquet or sling is suddenly required. Incidentally, did you know this place is supposed to be haunted?'

'I have heard tales to that effect.'

'One of the students thinks she has seen a monk dragging a sack. She wanted me to ask you whether she could come for psychiatric treatment but of course I fobbed her off.'

'Why?'

'Well, you don't run a private practice any more. I explained she'd have to go to London and attend your clinic, but that, even if she did, she wouldn't see you.'

'What is her name?'

'I don't know. I wasn't going to ask, anyway, but, as soon as I'd given her the bird, a surge of strawberry-seekers rolled up and I saw no more of her. It was after that that I explored around a bit and had my swim.'

'I am interested in this girl because Miss Peterson, the Senior Tutor, told me the same story.'

'So the girl had been to her for help and consolation?'

'Oh, no, nothing like that. I meant that she herself has seen the ghost. Only being older and more sceptical she regards him merely as a prowler, so now, at nights, the College is under police protection.'

'Well, in a women's college, I suppose a prowler is even more worrying than a ghost. You hear some pretty lurid tales these days about nurses' homes, women's hostels, single girls' bed-sitters and the like. What did the Senior Tutor think she saw? Somebody at dinner mentioned a monk.'

'The Senior Tutor, more reasonably, thought it was a man wearing a white anorak with the hood pulled over his head.'

'Is this fairly recent?'

'Apparently. There are other stories, though. It seems that there is what may be called a permanent wager offered among the students. Did you visit the cloister on your perambulations?'

'Yes. Not a place in which I should care to spend much time. It's the sort of set-up immortalised in *La Belle au Bois Dormant*, all overgrown with unpruned rambler roses. It's dark and smells damp and if there *is* a ghost here, that's where I'd say it walks.'

'You would be right, I daresay. This wager to which I referred. . .'

'. . .Is to walk widdershins three times slowly round the cloister at the witching hour of midnight on All Hallows Eve. I was hearing about it at dinner. One of the dons told me that she took on the bet once when she was a student, but didn't win it because after the first time round she turned and fled. She said she didn't actually *see* anything, but she felt that something was *following* her all the time.'

'Another student playing a trick on her, I imagine.'

'She said nobody would do such a thing. She added that she wouldn't take on the bet again for a thousand pounds. But what about the Senior Tutor? You said she saw something, too.'

'Yes, indeed she did, but it had disappeared before she could decide whether it was real or some trick of the moonlight.'

'If it's really a Peeping Tom they ought to form a posse, waylay him and chuck him in the river.'

'He would pollute the water, perhaps. We are not to leave tomorrow until after lunch so if you set eyes on your worried student during the morning, you might waylay her and ask her to talk to me.'

Apart from the High Mistress's Lodging, the refectory and the chapel, the only other remains of the mediaeval buildings to be in daily use were the Senior Common room and its buttery. These, as they had once been part of the abbess's lodging, were conveniently situated in that members of the Senior Common room did not need to cross the grounds to attend Hall or chapel unless they were in their own rooms in the new buildings; also the Senior Commonroom gave direct access to the Fellows' garden.

It was not from the Senior Commonroom, however, that Miss Peterson claimed to have seen the prowler, but from the same part of the new buildings as, it turned out, the student had seen what she claimed to be the ghost of a monk.

Miss Peterson had left College in her car immediately after the dinner following the garden-party, and so could not be questioned further, but the student, whose name was Runmede, was waylaid by Laura as she came out from breakfast and invited to stroll with Dame Beatrice in the grounds.

'I am told that you are psychic,' said Dame Beatrice, when they met, 'and that you wished to tell me of your experiences.'

'I only want to be sure I'm not going mad,' said the girl. 'There has always been something mystical about moonlight and one does remember that the word *lunatic* comes from *luna*. Besides, moonlight and magic are closely connected, aren't they? By moonlight Medea gathered the enchanted herbs that did renew old Aeson. Then, of course, there is Oberon's contention that he and Titania were ill-met by moonlight. Also, it's rather easy to fall in love by moonlight.'

'Yes, indeed,' said Dame Beatrice.

'It was seeing him the second time that worried me,' went on the student, 'because that time it wasn't any trick of shadows; he was there, out in Bessie's Quad, right in the open, and he only existed down to his waist.'

'As somebody once said of Mr Rochester.'

'He was dragging something heavy in a sack,' said the student, ignoring the slur on the hero of Jane Eyre.

'How tall did he seem?' asked Dame Beatrice.

'I couldn't say. My room is on the top floor of New Building, so, as I was looking down, I can't say how tall he was. Anyway, as I was trying to tell you, he had no legs. He was in white, with his cowl drawn over his head, and then, from the waist downward, he simply didn't exist. It was very frightening. Then he disappeared. That's how I know I saw a ghost. He just disappeared.'

'Both times?'

'Yes.'

'Later on perhaps you will be good enough to show me the spot at which he vanished. By the way, did you think he might have come from the river?'

'The river? Well, I suppose he *could* have done, but I don't really think so, because each time he was coming from the direction of Bessie's Quad, and that doesn't suggest the river, does it?'

'And he had his back to you both times?'

'No, he was sideways on, in profile, only I couldn't see a face because of his hood, but whether he was subjective or objective, well, I'd be ever so relieved if you could tell me.'

'Oh, I can tell you that you weren't seeing things, as the vulgar express it. The Senior Tutor, Miss Peterson, is your witness. She also saw the ghost, although she prefers to call him a prowler.'

'Oh, dear! That's not very nice, either. I'm not sure I wouldn't rather he were a ghost,' said Miss Runmede, looking very much alarmed. Dame Beatrice reassured her.

'Have no fear. Miss Peterson made a report and the grounds are patrolled every night. What a very pleasant quadrangle this is.'

'Yes, the flowers in the borders *are* agreeable, but have you seen the little secluded garden we call the Abbess's Walk? I think it's the most charming spot of all. Do let me show you.' It seemed that Dame Beatrice's words had had a heartening effect on the student. She spoke blithely.

The Abbess's Walk was indeed a charming spot. It was only about forty yards long and fifteen yards wide, but its intriguing little stone-flagged paths were bordered by lavender, antirrhinums, foxgloves and larkspur and there was a background of grey stone walls. As well as the cottage-garden flowers there were white, yellow and red roses whose scent out-vied the lavender in filling the enclosed air with fragrance; but what intrigued Dame Beatrice more than the old-world garden itself, delightful though she found it, was the fact that it communicated at one end, by means of a wicket-gate, with the main quadrangle and, at the other, with no barrier of any kind, with the cloister.

'I wonder whether we might perambulate the cloister?' she suggested.

'Yes, of course. There's nothing much to see except the roses and they're all over the place. The cloister is hardly ever used, so I suppose the gardeners don't pay it all that much attention. They've plenty of other things to do in the quads and in the High Mistress's and the Fellows' gardens. There's been talk of training back the roses and of putting a lily-pond in the middle of the cloister garth and last term the digging was begun, but I don't think they've touched it this summer.'

The cloister, as Laura had discovered, was dark and damp. The unglazed, fourteenth-century openings which, on all four sides, overlooked the untidy, grassy square of the cloister garth, were indeed smothered and almost covered up by the roses whose growth had become out of hand. There was only one way of leaving the cloister itself – to walk out on to its garth, but this opening must have been almost impassable because of the roses except that recently some secateurs had been at work on the more obstinate and choking of the stems so that a way through could be made.

Risking a scratched face and hands, Dame Beatrice pushed past the formidable trails and approached an excavation in the centre of the untidy square of grass. The student followed her.

'Hullo,' she said. 'The workmen must have been here again and partly filled in the hole they dug. I wonder what made them do that?'

'Yes, they have now made it much too shallow for the purpose of sinking a pool for water-lilies and other aquatic plants,' commented Dame Beatrice, studying the excavation. She glanced at her watch. 'Dear me! I must go and get ready for lunch. I wonder whether you would do one more thing for me if you can spare the time this afternoon?'

'Of course, Dame Beatrice.'

'Show me your room and the window from which you saw the ghost, and also perhaps you would indicate, as exactly as you can, where the prowler made his appearances. On which floor would Miss Peterson's room be, I wonder?'

'The dons and Fellows occupy the ground floor.'

'So Miss Peterson may have had a better view of this nocturnal visitor than you had. May I ask why you were up so late when you saw what you took to be the ghost?'

'The first time it was because I couldn't sleep. I'd been crossed in love. The second time it was because I was sublimating by writing a poem about my miseries. That always seems to make one feel better about things, I find.'

'Ah, yes, I quite understand,' said Dame Beatrice.

CHAPTER 6

Owl-call hollow round the silent house

Lunch was in the High Mistress's lodging and, in addition to Dame Beatrice and Laura, the guests were the Chief Constable of the county and a cousin to the High Mistress, a redhaired man of forty named Fairlie.

'I want to thank you, Gerald,' said the High Mistress, at a pause in the conversation, 'for the very unobtrusive and courteous way in which your policemen carried out their duties in Bessie's Quad yesterday and for the comfort it is to know that we are protected at night.'

'Not really *my* policemen,' the Chief Constable pointed out. 'Chief Superintendent Nicholl is the chap, and a very good chap he is. Actually he's on a murder case at present. At least, we think it's murder, although it may just be that the young woman has staged a disappearance.'

'Not a Miss Coralie St Malo, by any chance?' asked Dame Beatrice.

'How on earth did you guess that, Beatrice?' asked the Chief Constable, with whom she had been acquainted for many years, having known his mother since their university days when the latter had been an undergraduate and Dame Beatrice a lecturer in medical jurisprudence.

'It was not so much a guess as a deduction, my dear Gerald. When one hears certain facts, one is apt to draw certain conclusions.'

The Chief Constable looked uneasily at Laura and then said to his hostess.

'Certain matters have come to our knowledge which reflect no credit on the nephew of a certain distinguished member of this University, so we should wish our activities in the matter to remain as unremarked as possible at present. We may be barking up quite the wrong tree. If we are, well, the more we keep ourselves in the background, the better.'

'I shall be as dumb as the Eldest Oyster,' said the High Mistress, 'so do tell us what it's all about.'

'Mrs Gavin is entirely in my confidence,' said Dame Beatrice, 'and knows all that I know. But if I may put a question to you before the subject, as might be desirable, can be changed, how do the police come to know anything of the matter?'

'Nicholl received what is known as a tip-off from one of the Waynefléte College servants. I don't know why these worn-out theories are still extant.'

'What theories? Are they documented?' asked the High Mistress, smiling.

'The theories that the College servants have neither eyes nor ears, let alone feelings.'

'I don't think that applies to the scouts in the women's colleges.'

'Probably not, but some of the male dons appear to think we're back in the early nineteenth century. They make no allowance at all for the fact that in these days Jack not only thinks he's as good as his master, but, in many cases, actually earns more money.'

'I should not think that would apply to the scouts here, either. I don't think we pay them nearly enough for what they do.'

'I was speaking in general terms. However, to return to the special subject under discussion, it appears that this particular scout had taken umbrage over some triviality or other – the disappearance of some bottles of wine, I believe.'

'Scarcely a trivial matter with wine the price it is since the last budget,' said Laura.

'Well, at any rate, the Warden's nephew, a man named Lawrence, appears to have accused the scout in front of the College Bursar. The case was disproved, but the man seems to have been determined upon some form of revenge. Apparently he had overheard part of a conversation involving a woman he knew, a woman who used her stage name of Coralie St Malo, although he knew her as a Miss Piggen. Anyhow, the fellow seems to have come to the conclusion that it was a clandestine assignment, since he could think of no good reason for a meeting between Lawrence who, after all, is the Warden of Wayneflete's nephew, and a girl from Headman's Lane. He decided that it might be interesting to follow up the matter, so he sneaked along and was a witness of the meeting at a public house between Lawrence and this woman. It was the second time he had seen them together, the first having been in the market, where he overheard their conversation.'

'So the Wayneflete College scout had known the young woman,' said Dame Beatrice.

'She had lived in the next street from his. It's rather a poor quarter of the town and Headman's Lane is not the most salubrious part of it, even at that. The residents in his own street regard themselves as a cut above the Laneites. That is why he thought there was something very fishy about Lawrence's getting together with the girl in a public house so far out of the town. But what do *you* know about Coralie St Malo, Beatrice?'

'Oh, I heard her name mentioned some week or so ago,' said Dame Beatrice evasively. 'Did the College servant gain anything from his eavesdropping?'

'He claims that he was a witness of the public house meeting. It began cordially, but degenerated into a quarrel. He was in the public bar, but the two met in the saloon bar. However, the counters are at right angles to one another so that, at slack times, one barman or barmaid can attend to both. He was in a strategic position, therefore, for a little spying and eavesdropping. He seems, from what he overheard, to have come to the conclusion that the woman was demanding some kind of compensation. He assumed that it was for breach of promise of marriage, for she said that if she did not obtain satisfaction she (in her own words, according to this fellow) would know what to do about it.'

'Well,' said the High Mistress, 'Mr Lawrence could hardly give her one sort of satisfaction, seeing that he is already married to the Dean's secretary.'

'He told my son that it was to one of your dons,' said Dame Beatrice. 'He must be a man of shallow character if snobbishness of that sort is part of his make-up.'

'Under present conditions, Miss St Malo might be unwise to invoke the law over a question of compensation,' said the redhaired Fairlie, pursuing his own train of thought, 'especially if there were no witnesses to an offer of marriage. I don't know much about that side of the law, but I do know that breach of promise cases don't by any means always succeed, especially nowadays.'

'In this instance,' said Dame Beatrice, 'it was not a question of breach of promise in the sense that you mean.'

The others looked at her, but she added nothing to this statement. The Chief Constable went on with his story.

'Apparently, by the time they left the public house, the quarrel had been resolved, for Lawrence drove the woman in his own car to her lodging-house. The scout, who had gone to their rendezvous on his motorcycle, followed them. Lawrence and the girl went to the house in Headman's Lane and the man says he waited outside for an hour, but Lawrence did not emerge, so he went to his own home, intending to call upon Miss St Malo on the following morning to find out what he could and, presumably, to cut himself in on any deal which might have been made between the two parties. I suppose he intended to offer to support Miss St Malo's claim if his deductions as to a possible breach of promise action proved to be correct.'

'You said that this man lived in her neighbourhood, but how well did he know Miss St Malo?' asked Dame Beatrice.

'That is one of the things we have to find out. However, to go on with the man's story, it appears that he did call on the following morning, only to find nobody at home.'

'Why wasn't he about his College duties?'

'Oh, didn't I mention that? The fellow had taken so much umbrage over the accusation of having stolen the wine that he had handed in his notice, so for the time under consideration he was unemployed.'

'With leisure to make as much mischief as he could,' said Laura.

'That's it. He says he called several times on Miss St Malo after that, but she was not in residence. He questioned the other residents, but nobody had seen her leave, so he states that he thought it his duty to contact the police because of the quarrel in the pub and the threats he had heard the woman utter. We made enquiries and we turned up a very significant fact. Lawrence and Miss St Malo were married twelve years ago at a registrar's office in Portsmouth and we can find no evidence that they were ever divorced.'

'But that is impossible!' exclaimed the High Mistress. 'As I said, he is married to the Dean's secretary.'

'Well, he may be married to her *now*,' said the Chief Constable drily, 'but he wasn't a few weeks ago, not legally anyway, because then this St Malo woman was still alive and we can prove it.'

'You have nothing, then, except this servant's somewhat tainted evidence, to indicate that she is not alive at this moment,' said Dame Beatrice.

'The fact remains that she has disappeared from her lodging, and that the last time she was seen was in company with Lawrence. Then there was the demand for money and a quarrel.'

'Are there any other witnesses, apart from this disgruntled manservant?' asked Dame Beatrice.

'The barmaid at the public house remembers the quarrel. It was too early in the evening for the bar to be much patronised, so she noticed the couple particularly, and states that they seemed ill-assorted. In her own words, 'him being quite the gentleman and her as common as muck'. However, she also states that the man talked the woman round, bought her a second drink and that they left the bar apparently on friendly terms. Later, two women who have rooms in the same lodginghouse as Miss St Malo saw her come back that same evening with a man, but this was so common an occurrence that they were not even interested and cannot describe the man. Miss St Malo seems to have done a moonlight flit, however.'

Lunch over, Dame Beatrice and Laura took the path between the High Mistress's and the Fellows' gardens and reached Bessie's Quad. Here they found the student awaiting them. Laura went over to where she had parked the car on the previous afternoon and Dame Beatrice greeted Miss Runmede.

'I do hope you have not been waiting long,' she said. 'I don't want to take up too much of your time, but I am more than ever interested in your ghostly prowler. I wonder whether you will be kind enough to show me exactly where he was on the occasions on which you saw him?'

'Yes, of course I will.'

'And, after that, if you have no objection, I should like to be taken to the window from which you observed him.'

'Well,' said Miss Runmede, when the two ghost-walks were completed, 'that's as near as I can remember, but it seems very different by daylight and of course it's different from down here. I was high up in the building when I saw him each time.'

'Yes, of course. I am very greatly obliged to you. Have no further fear. I am convinced that nobody will ever see the prowler again. In any case, as I told you, you are not the only person to have seen him, therefore steps have been taken.'

'You wanted me to show you where I think he disappeared. Why?'

'Because, from what you have shown me, I think your prowler, wearing a white anorak or some other kind of white jacket over dark trousers, entered the Abbess's Walk from the main quadrangle and that is why he seemed to disappear. He then, I think, went into the cloisters and left by the way you took me to visit them first of all. I want to go to your window to determine whether, if that is what he did, you would or would not have been able to witness his departure.'

They mounted uncarpeted stone steps until they reached the top-floor landing. Here a long, bare corridor, interspersed with white-painted doors bearing names slotted into metal holders, indicated those who slept in each of the rooms.

'Not so different from what the convent itself was like, I suppose,' said Miss Runmede, producing a key and unlocking the door which bore her name.

'Not so different from a present-day convent, perhaps,' said Dame Beatrice, surveying the somewhat Spartan simplicity of the room which, except for a bookcase, a good copy of Jan Molenaer's *Two Boys and a Girl Making Music* and a few family photographs, was bare to the point of austerity, 'but very different, I think, from the long, cold dorters or dormitories of the Middle Ages. The passage lacks, too, the stair into the church for night prayers'.

She established herself at the window. 'Would Miss Peterson's room be directly below this one?' she asked.

'Not quite, but near enough. She shares a scout with Miss Hastings and Miss Hastings's rooms back on to Miss Peterson's. In fact, her sitting-room is exactly below this room, but looks out the other way.'

'So Miss Hastings would not have seen your ghost?'

'Not unless she was in Miss Peterson's room talking to her and looking out of her window, but I don't think even the dons sit up as late as two o'clock in the morning.'

When she and Laura were on their way home that afternoon, Dame Beatrice said: 'Tell me, did you ever know of workmen enthusiastic enough to do too much digging and then have to fill in part of the excavation they had laboured so hard to make?'

'Oh, you mean that mess they've left in the middle of the cloister garth at Abbesses College. What has turned your mind in that particular direction?' Laura asked.

'Miss Runmede's reference to the sack which appears to have aroused your interest. That earth in the cloister garth has been disturbed quite recently.'

'And you don't think that was done by honest British workmen? You malign the hardworking fellows!'

'That may or may not be so. All the same, I have suggested to the Chief Constable that an investigation of the cloister garth at Abbesses College might yield spectacular although macabre results. What with the report of a quarrel, with or without a reconciliation, Miss Runmede's ghost, Miss Peterson's prowler, and the apparent disappearance of Miss St Malo, I am wondering whether the surname of the apparition is Lawrence.'

'I wonder whether Miss Peterson spotted the sack?'

'I think that if Miss Peterson had noticed the sack she would have reported it.'

'The idea would be that she saw the prowler the first night he came, but not the second.'

'What makes you say that? It could be the other way round, could it not?'

'Well, assuming – as I take it we are assuming – that the sack contained a body, I should imagine that the murderer came the first time to spy out the lie of the land and the second time to dispose of the contents of the sack.'

'We are assuming, then, that it was the same man both times. That, I think, is likely, although not, of course, certain. As for your theory concerning the two visits, is it not just as likely that it was on the first one that he got rid of the body and that the second visit was to make sure that all was well? However, the matter can soon be settled. Get Abbesses College on the telephone and ask the porter to put you through to the New Buildings, so that you can speak to Miss Runmede. She should still be in College.'

'She may be out for the evening,' said Laura, going to the telephone. Miss Runmede, however, was working in her room and was soon answering the call. She was certain that the man had had the sack with him on the first occasion only.

'It sounds now as though he was a burglar,' she said, 'but, if so, why should he appear from Bessie's Quad? You can't get in that way once the gatehouse portal is locked. Have they arrested him?'

'Not yet. You mentioned two o'clock in the morning and that it was at the same hour, approximately, that you saw him each time.'

'More or less. I remember hearing a clock strike and I hate hearing a clock strike at night. It sounds so sinister – "for whom the bell tolls" and all that.'

'And it was moonlight both times, you stated.'

'Moonlight and a clear sky, but even if they catch him, I couldn't possibly identify him for the reasons I gave you.'

'So what now?' asked Laura, later.

'Nothing. I have drawn the Chief Constable's attention to the excavation in the cloister garth, and have told him that the man was dragging a sack. We can do no more.'

PART TWO

Seepage in the Cellar

CHAPTER 7

The hastily-rigged machinery of the law

Chief Superintendent Nicholl was a man of slow thought, but once an idea had lodged itself firmly in his mind he took immediate action. From the moment he had been told that a prowler had been spotted after midnight in the grounds of Abbesses College he had seen to it that two of his men were stationed on duty with reliefs every two hours. One was to remain in view of the gatehouse and Bessie's Quad, the other to be on patrol duty around the grounds. They would remain until the arrival of the porter in the morning.

The news which he received from the Chief Constable following the luncheon at the High Mistress's lodging urged him to take further measures, but he retained his bump of caution and proceeded with care.

The first thing he did was to ring up the firm of contractors who had undertaken to establish the lily-pond in the middle of the cloister garth. Their address he obtained from the senior porter. They were not a local firm, but were domiciled in Reading.

The job, he was told, would have been finished during the College vacation following the Lent term which had ended in the last week of March, except for the fact that the Lady Bursar (complained the manager with resigned but scathing emphasis) kept changing her mind. First she wanted a concrete pond, but then she demurred on the score of expense. Then she settled (or so the firm thought) for a pre-fabricated arrangement in glass fibre but, shown a specimen, was not certain that it would meet with her requirements as it was 'not quite what she had thought of'.

Finally the workmen had excavated to the required depth for a green-painted, metal, kidney-shaped container of more or less the size she specified, but work was held up again when she discovered that to bring the vessel from the cloister into the garth would involve removing stone from two narrow arches, one giving admittance to the cloister itself and the other leading out of the cloister on to the square of grass it enclosed.

'So there we are and there we're stuck until she finally makes up her mind,' said the manager, when he was interviewed by the Chief Superintendent, later.

'So anybody could have known all about this job,' said Nicholl.

'I suppose so, if they'd visited the College. Some parts of it, I dare say, are open to the public during vacations.'

'And this hole of yours...'

'Begun in the third week of March and we should have had the whole job finished by the time the students came back at the beginning of April. The Lent vacation is a short one, but quite long enough for a little job like that, especially when we thought the lady had settled on a pre-fab pool. She planned to plant the lilies and things herself, you see. We had only to sink the pond.'

'I've been along to the site. Your men don't seem to have put up a workmen's hut of any kind. I suppose it wasn't necessary.'

'Not really. We did suggest a hut, if only so that the men could have somewhere to leave their tools, but the lady pointed out that there was shelter in the cloister which of course we couldn't gainsay. It was quite evident that she didn't intend to let us put up a hut. She pointed out that it would spoil the amenities as far as visitors were concerned and that the excavation itself was eyesore enough. She is a very difficult, masterful lady and you can't get the better of her.'

'You never thought of suggesting that she should take her contract elsewhere, I suppose?'

'Well, we'd already begun our excavation in preparation for the pool before all these difficulties cropped up. Also – well, we rather wanted to be able to put on our prospectus and our advertisements that we were contractors to the University.'

'Were the same men employed all the time on this particular job?'

'Oh, yes. Even without any mechanical aid – impossible, of course, in such an enclosed spare – it was only a three-day job for three chaps and a wheelbarrow.'

'I'd like to speak to those men and, more than that, I'd like to take them along to look at the excavation with me.'

'Why? Anything wrong? Somebody been burying a body?' asked the manager jovially. His face altered when Nicholl replied that his guess was as good as the next man's and that stranger things had been known to happen.

'Look here, now,' the manager said anxiously, 'I mean, my chaps are in the clear, I hope?'

'No reason to suspect them and of course yours and mine may be nothing but wild guesses. I hope they are,' said Nicholl. 'Anyway don't broadcast them.'

The workmen were named Bob, Ernie and Bert. Assured by Nicholl that nothing to their detriment was involved, they abandoned their first determination to 'get our Union on to this,' and (reluctantly on their part, even on the assurance of the head of the firm that their day's pay was not in jeopardy) they were taken in police cars to Abbesses College.

Their comments were illuminating. Their first care was to inspect their tools. These had been stored in a dark corner of the cloister in readiness for a resumption of operations.

'Them ent our tools,' said Ernie. Bob was less precipitate.

'I reckon them's our tools,' he said, 'but not where we left 'em. Clean my shovel was, too and all. Look at her now!' The excavation, when the men had ducked under the archway which was still partly choked by the trailing rose-stems, also came in for criticism. 'That ent the way us left un. Somebody ben mucken around wi' her, I reckon,' Bob averred.

'Ah,' said Nicholl, 'that's so, is it? I suppose you're sure?'

Bert, who had not, so far, committed himself to speech, grunted a mild oath and spat into the excavation. The others, with similar oral embellishment but without the added emphasis of expectoration, declared that they were certain.

'Know the look of your own job when you sees her again,' added Bob.

'Right. That's what we wanted to know. Well, I'm afraid we're going to muck up your job still further, but we'll make it all right with your firm.'

'Struck oil, have us?' asked Ernie, with heavy irony.

'You never know,' replied Nicholl. He sent them home in one of the police cars, and the remaining couple of his men, having returned to the cloister to impound two of the shovels, removed their tunics and rolled up their shirt-sleeves.

The already twice-worked soil was light and easy to shift, but even so they sweated for nearly three-quarters of an hour before they uncovered and retrieved the sack with its grisly contents.

'The Lady Bursar didn't bargain for the answer to all her shilly-shallying about what kind of pond she wanted,' said the Chief Superintendent, reporting to the Chief Constable later. 'If she'd made up her mind at the beginning to have the concrete basin instead of belly-aching about the cost and so on, we'd never have had a body, never in this life. That unfinished hole was an open invitation to a murderer.'

'Yes, if the murderer knew the hole was there, and that throws the whole thing wide open. It isn't possible to check on all the people who visited the College between the time the excavation was abandoned and the time that prowler with the sack was spotted in the grounds of the College.'

'Let alone that we can't be sure that that particular sack contained the body, sir.'

'True. It's proof presumptive, but not proof positive.'

'It's just over a week since the student and this lecturer spotted the prowler. Added to that, there's no confirmation of the student's story that the man was dragging a sack. The lecturer didn't see it.'

'But she only saw the chap once, so that isn't important.'

'The next thing is to get the body identified, assuming (without prejudice, of course) that it's this woman, Coralie St Malo.'

'Because she's disappeared it doesn't follow that she's dead. She may have skipped her digs just because she couldn't pay the rent. It's a chancy kind of life for these chorus and bit-part people, I believe.'

'Yes, there's that. Well, we'd better get hold of Lawrence and see whether he recognises her. There was that row in the pub, sir. It could be a pointer.'

'I suggest, as she was found on their premises, we try the College authorities first. If she's who you think she might be, nobody here will recognise her, so then we can get on to Lawrence, although it's chancing our arm a bit.'

'Not a very nice job for these College ladies. She's not the prettiest of sights, sir.'

'We'll try the College porters, then. They won't be quite so squeamish and they may have spotted some suspicious character about the place. I wonder how the fellow got in after dark?'

CHAPTER 8

The lie in the twisted thought that
travesties the truth

'Hullo, what's this?' said Laura. She was sorting out the morning's correspondence and the question was rhetorical. From a foolscap envelope she extracted a typed letter and, with it, a clipping from a newspaper. She was perusing the clipping when her employer came down to breakfast. She looked up from her reading.

'The fun seems to be under way,' she said. 'I opened this envelope because it was typewritten, but it's from the Chief Constable and I think the contents are for your personal information. The newspaper bit is all about that cloister garth at Abbesses College. They've found a body in it and the police are calling upon a man to assist them in their enquiries. I bet that means Lawrence!'

'So you suppose him to have killed his redundant first wife, do you? I would not have associated him with physical violence, but perhaps you are right.'

'But there's an odd thing about it. The body has been identified as that of the *second* wife, the secretary to the Dean of Abbesses.'

'Interesting. Are there any details?'

'Only that she'd been dead for some days before the body was buried. The police are still looking for the place where she actually died. I don't suppose they'll make an arrest until they find it. They haven't found the weapon either.'

'What of Coralie St Malo? Has *she* been found?'

'She's been traced to Blackpool, where she's with a pier-head concert-party. She's been sharing a room with another chorus girl there.'

'So the story of the public-house quarrel between Miss St Malo and Lawrence is entirely irrelevant, although their subsequent reconciliation (if both stories are true) may not be irrelevant at all.'

'You mean Lawrence may have ditched the Dean's secretary, in the most permanent manner known to man, in preparation for taking up again with Coralie?'

'Nothing, on the face of it, seems less likely, unless there are wheels within wheels of which we know nothing.'

'What kind of wheels would those be?'

'Square ones, perhaps.'

'Are you proposing to take a hand in the matter?'

'Not unless I am called in officially when the police have made an arrest, so that I can report upon the state of mind of the accused.'

'But you were the first person to see that there was something suspicious about that hole in the middle of the cloister garth.'

'And you were the first person to hear about the prowler with the sack. Are *you* proposing to conduct an investigation?'

Laura looked down her nose, but had no need to reply to the facetious question, for at that moment the telephone rang and she went into the hall to answer it.

'It was the High Mistress of Abbesses College,' she said, coming back into the room. 'She's in no end of a taking. The police have given up questioning Lawrence, it seems, and have taken the two College porters into custody. Will you speak to her? I asked her to hold on.'

The High Mistress begged Dame Beatrice to come and see her.

The High Mistress may have been in a state of great disquiet, as Laura, in other words, had indicated, but if so she did not betray it when she received her visitors. She was a dumpling of a woman with intelligent eyes, a fighter's nose and a good humoured mouth which, however, could betray rat-trap determination when occasion called for it.

She greeted Dame Beatrice and Laura with great cordiality and gave them tea. Her parlourmaid – a distinction must be made here: the dons and the students had scouts to attend on them, but the servants at the Lodging were always referred to as the maids – her parlourmaid cleared the table at the end of a meal during which the conversation had simply consisted of general chit-chat, and then the High Mistress got down to business.

'Poor Oates and Wagstaffe,' she said. 'Two more law-abiding men have never lived. To accuse them of stealing is more than monstrous; it is utterly ridiculous! And then to charge them with murdering the person they are supposed to have robbed – well, words fail me!'

'On what is the charge based, then?' Dame Beatrice enquired.

'The police searched Mrs Lawrence's rooms and then the College. The actual murder was committed, it seems, in the gatehouse cellar. It appears that there was some kind of fuss going on between Mrs Lawrence and the porters over a missing parcel which was reported to have been left at the lodge but which did not materialise. I knew about it, because the porters had complained of Mrs Lawrence's insinuations that one of them had stolen it. They spoke to the Dean first and she referred them to me. I heard their complaint and then I spoke to Mrs Lawrence. In point of fact, the College pays my own secretary, the Bursar's and the Dean's, and although we have a voice in the appointments we are not permitted to terminate them without the consent of the governing body. That, needless to say, would in practice never be refused, but that is by the way.'

'So, the alleged motive having been suggested, we come to a matter of means and opportunity, together with the dates when these would have been available. The means, according to the newspaper report, were economical and hideous,' said Dame Beatrice.

'Yes, the poor woman's throat was cut.'

'And the opportunity for somebody to cut it?'

'Oh,' said the High Mistress grimly, 'in a place like the cellar under the gatehouse there would be opportunity enough. It is hardly ever used except by Mrs Lawrence herself.'

'Must be an awful lot of blood about in the cellar,' said Laura.

'I suppose there's no question of suicide? People do cut their own throats. We've got books on forensic medicine at the Stone House. Some of the photographs in them are pretty horrible and most of them are of suicides.'

'I really don't care to discuss it,' said Dr Durham-Basing. 'What I do care about are those two unfortunate men. I am as convinced of their innocence as I am of my own. I refer, of course, to the disappearance of Mrs Lawrence's parcel. The graver charge surely cannot really be sustained, but if we can disprove theft, a charge of murder falls to the ground automatically, for it disposes of the motive.'

'The police must have some grounds for suspecting them, even vaguely, of murder,' Dame Beatrice suggested.

'Unsafe grounds, in my opinion. They claim that, apart from myself and the senior members of the College, nobody except the porters has a key to the gate. The gatehouse cellar can be reached only from inside our walls, you see.'

'Have they considered the possibility of access to the College buildings by way of the river?' asked Dame Beatrice. 'Laura thought that a light skiff, for example, could be pulled ashore and transported round the barrier which shuts off your private stretch of the river from the rest of the stream. From what Miss Runmede has told us, it seems that the prowler she saw must have come from Bessie's Quad, but that need not rule out the possibility that he came across from the opposite direction.'

'I will see what I can find out about that. The barrier you speak of is supposed to be sufficient to ensure our privacy. The last thing I could countenance would be that we should be open to invasion from the town or from any of the men's Colleges.'

'Who identified the body?' asked Dame Beatrice.

'The porters were called upon first of all. The formal identification was carried out by Mrs Lawrence's brother, a Mr Bill Caret.'

'Not by Lawrence himself?'

'Before the inquest was held, Lawrence was already being questioned by the police. By the time he had proved his alibi and been released, the body had been buried – formally, this time, of course.'

'His alibi, I take it, was provided by the Warden of Wayneflete College.'

'No. Mr Lawrence was no longer staying with his uncle. I do not know who was responsible for his alibi.'

'Coralie St Malo, I expect,' said Laura to Dame Beatrice, when they had left the High Mistress and were on their way to the Chief Constable's house where, as the result of a telephone call from the High Mistress's Lodging requesting an interview with him, they were to dine. 'By the way, my question about suicide didn't get answered.'

'It hardly needed to be put.'

'You mean that, even if she did kill herself, she could hardly have put herself in a sack and buried herself. Oh, well – damn silly question, etcetera,' admitted Laura.

The Chief Constable himself raised the question of suicide as soon as dinner was over.

'Of course, even if the body had not been put in a sack and even if it had not been buried, we should have ruled out suicide,' he said. 'According to the medical evidence, suicides who intend to cut their own throats – and it's not an uncommon method of terminating a life which has become intolerable to its owner – they invariably make some tentative incisions before they nerve themselves to do the actual deed. Anything up to a dozen or more of these preliminary dividings of the skin are common, I'm told. There was nothing of the sort in this case. The doctors think she was gripped by the hair from behind, her head pulled back and one great slash made right across the thyro-hyoid ligament. They suggest that the slash was carried out by a right-handed person.'

'What made the police, in the beginning, suspect Lawrence?'

'Husbands are always the prime suspects in cases of murder when neither rape nor robbery is involved. More particularly in this case, we thought he might have been able at some time to take an impression of his wife's key to the College entrance and also that, because of her, he could have known of the excavation in which she was buried.'

'And who provided him with an alibi?'

'His landlady in his own university town of Norcaster. Unless her evidence is cooked up and false, it doesn't seem that Lawrence can be our man.'

'You know when the murder was committed, then?'

'Within limits, and those limits are confidently covered by his landlady's statement.'

'I see. And what about the accused men, Oates and Wagstaffe?'

'Apart from Lawrence himself, they not only fulfil all the requirements, but are even more vulnerable than, after we had questioned him, we thought Lawrence was. They – or one of them – had a motive which, in Lawrence's case, did not exist. Apparently Mrs Lawrence had been making herself very unpleasant to the porters over a missing parcel. She seems to have been a very plain-spoken young woman.'

'If we might return to the subject of Oates and Wagstaffe, do you suppose them to have been in collusion over the murder?'

'One could have been accessory to the other, but that will sort itself out sooner or later. We believe the murder was committed by one man only, but at the moment we cannot eliminate either Oates or Wagstaffe because, after the lapse of time between the murder and the discovery of the body, the medical evidence of time of death can only be approximate. As you probably know, the porters' hours of duty alternate. They work a shift system in the porters' lodge from eight in the morning until midnight, four hours on and four hours off duty. They sleep in their own homes, which are less than a stone's throw from the College and are, in fact, two semi-detached cottages, both of them College property so that the porters live rent free. The College is well endowed, thanks to the generosity of a former student, and the porters' jobs are exceptionally well paid.'

'So that the men who had charge of the lodge would stand to lose excellent wages and rent-free accommodation if a charge of theft was proved against them,' said Laura.

'Exactly. It makes a powerful motive for getting rid of their accuser.'

'But I thought the High Mistress had refused to entertain the theory that the missing parcel had been stolen by the porters,' said Dame Beatrice. 'What was in it, I wonder?'

'According to Mrs Lawrence, when she called in the police, a gold repeater watch with a *repoussé* case very elegantly moulded with a scene of Greek nymphs. It had a *champlevé* dial and the hall-mark of 1724. A very valuable piece indeed.'

'You appear to have memorised its perfections,' said Dame Beatrice.

'I'm interested in clocks and watches and have a small collection of my own, so I was particularly interested.'

'What is a *repoussé* case?' asked Laura.

"Like anything else *repoussé*.'

'Oh, embossed. That accounts for the Greek nymphs, I suppose. And what is a *champlevé* dial? I'm sorry to be so ignorant.'

'Not at all. *Champlevé* is a technical term. It means that the dial of the watch has been cut away so that the numerals and other marks remain raised up.'

'Thank you. So what would such a watch be worth?'

'I could not say. Much would depend upon its condition.'

'Had Mrs Lawrence seen it before it disappeared?'

'No. She told us she had the description of it in a letter from the friend who sent it to her. She simply referred to him as 'Old Sir Anthony'. He wrote the letter to tell her that he was despatching the watch by registered post – or so she said.'

'So it was signed for,' said Dame Beatrice.

'Apparently not. The old gentleman must have omitted or forgotten to register the parcel. The porters contended that it had never turned up at all and the post office could not trace it.'

'And Mrs Lawrence affirmed that she had informed the porters that a parcel was to arrive for her?'

'Yes, but she described it as a *registered* parcel which, of course, owing to an oversight on the part, we think, of Sir Anthony himself, it was not. The servant would have registered it if he had been instructed to do so.'

'And there is no means of knowing which of the two porters was most likely to have taken it in if, indeed, it was ever delivered at the College?'

'No means at all. The man, Oates, clocks in at eight in the morning and goes off at twelve, so that if the parcel came by letter post which, as presumably it was small in bulk and not particularly heavy, it may well have done, Oates would have taken it in; but if it came by parcel post, it would not have arrived at the porters' lodge until between half-past two and half-past three in the afternoon, when Wagstaffe would have been on duty.'

'The porters were questioned at the time, I suppose?'

'Yes, but with a score or more parcels arriving every day for students and staff, they couldn't possibly be expected to remember any particular one, especially as nobody could tell them exactly which day or by which post it would have come, or give an exact description of it.'

'So nothing could be proved, yet the porters remained under suspicion.'

'Lambasted good and proper by Mrs Lawrence, one gathers,' said Laura.

'Until one or both of them got sick of it and did for her. Yes, I suppose that's about the size of it,' said the Chief Constable. 'It's not a clear-cut case by any means, though.'

Dame Beatrice and Laura left the Chief Constable's house at soon after nine and returned to the College and the High Mistress's Lodging to recount the details of the interview.

'How many people knew of the gatehouse cellar?' Dame Beatrice asked her.

'I suppose any number of people could have *known* of it, but only the porters and Mrs Lawrence had *keys* to it.'

'It was usually kept locked, then?'

'Yes. In these days one doesn't provide hidey-holes in a women's College.

'So why did Mrs Lawrence have a key?'

'She was a keen photographer and had permission to use part of the cellar as a darkroom.'

'And the porters?'

'The cellar used to be a prison for recalcitrant nuns, so it is divided into several small cells. Mrs Lawrence used the largest of these and the porters kept my garden-party deckchairs in the others.'

'So, if Mrs Lawrence was in her darkroom, the door to the cellar would not be locked.'

'As I've pointed out to the police, *anybody* bold enough to take the risk could have followed her down there, as the College grounds are open to daytime visitors. The fact that the porters had keys is therefore quite irrelevant, but the police can't get that missing parcel out of their obstinate heads and, of course, Mrs Lawrence had made herself *very* unpleasant about it.'

'The murderer, if you exonerate the porters, had to get into the College grounds by daylight, then. At what time of day did Mrs Lawrence use the darkroom?'

'In the evenings, after her secretarial duties were over. Oh, and in the daytime during the vacations, I suppose. She had a key to the main gate, just as my own secretary has.'

'Lawrence, of course, would have known of his wife's hobby and also that she had a key to the gate.'

'I suppose so, although I believe they were only together out of term-time. He was at his own university in term and she was here. It seemed an odd arrangement to me for a married couple, but no worse, I suppose, than being married to a sailor or both partners being on the stage.'

'Did Mrs Lawrence live in College?'

'No. She had rooms in the town, but very close at hand.'

'Did nobody realise she was missing? It seems to have been some time between the murder and the discovery of the body.'

'Nobody at all. Of course, when her body was found, her landlady was questioned, but she knew nothing. She had gone on holiday the week before College went down. She says that when she returned, a fortnight later, she assumed that Mrs Lawrence had gone on holiday, too, although she admitted she was a little surprised that Mrs Lawrence had not followed her usual practice of leaving a forwarding address for letters.'.

'At what time do you lock your gate at night?'

'At ten. The dons, as you know, have keys. Students on late passes have to ring for the porter, who is on duty until midnight. The bell connects with the Dean's quarters after that, so anybody coming back later than midnight has to be let in by the Dean and, unless there is a cast-iron reason for lateness, the offender is very likely to be rusticated.' She smiled and added, 'Even if only for getting the Dean out of bed. The students know the rules and, even in this undisciplined age, I do my best to see that those rules are kept. It's for the students' own good. They can't do their work if they are going to make whoopee at all hours of the night.'

It was arranged that the visitors should spend the night at the College. On their way home after breakfast on the following morning, Laura asked:

'Didn't you want to examine that gatehouse cellar for yourself?'

'With what object? The police will have searched it exhaustively and the floor and the walls will have been cleaned up long before this.'

'I wonder what made them think of looking there?'

'They would have been told about Mrs Lawrence's darkroom, no doubt, when the body was identified and they could get no help at her lodging.'

'Would anybody but the porters have moved the corpse, do you think? Surely any outsider would simply have left it to be found. It was taking an awful risk to drag it across to the cloister. Another thing: if Lawrence and his wife usually spent their holidays together, isn't it rather surprising that he doesn't seem to have reported that she was missing?'

'*If* they usually spent their holidays together it would be more than surprising; it would be incredible. However, we have no proof that they *were* accustomed to spend their holidays in each other's company.'

'Doctor Durham-Basing seemed to think they did.'

'Oh, no doubt the couple kept up appearances, but it need have been no more than that. According to what we know, Lawrence spent some part of his vacations with Sir Anthony and certainly did so this year.'

'With fatal results. I say, it does all hang together,' said Laura. 'I mean, if Mrs Lawrence knew that there had been funny business in connection with Sir Anthony's death and that Lawrence was coming in for a lot of money, money enough to get him out of the jam he was in...'

'Yes, but we cannot argue ahead of our data. Be patient, and let time pass,' said Dame Beatrice.

CHAPTER 9

We come to speak for the silent,
To be heard for the unheard,
To bear witness for one condemned.

'You know,' said Laura, 'I think the police have something up their sleeves. Surely the motive ascribed to the porters is inadequate? Men don't commit murder because they're accused of purloining a parcel, do they? It's not even as though a charge of theft has been proved.'

'I agree that the police may have more to go on than we have been told, but your second contention is more doubtful. The question of motive is a difficult one. That is why the courts are far more interested in means and opportunity than in motive, for it has often been shown that a motive for murder which might appear perfectly adequate to one person would never lead to such drastic repercussions in someone else. The point is beautifully made by H.R.F. Keating, you will remember, in his fascinating story *A Rush on the Ultimate.*'

'Yes, but that involved the game of croquet and it's well known that no other pastime, not even professional lawn tennis, arouses such bitter passions. There was no love lost between the English and American teenagers in *Little Women*, and what price the game of croquet in *Alice*?'

'Yes, indeed. If I remember the passage correctly. "Alice soon came to the conclusion that it was a very difficult game indeed. The players all played at once without waiting for turns, quarrelling all the while, and fighting for the hedgehogs." '

'Which were being used as croquet balls. Yes, and in a very short time the Queen was in a furious passion and went stamping about and shouting "Of with his head!" '

'It sounds very much like an acquaintance of mine. But, to return to our own particular sphere of interest, there is the important question of the parcel containing the watch. The most obvious point, it seems to me, is that there appears to be no real evidence that it was ever delivered to the College at all. If, however, it was despatched but did not arrive, it would be interesting to find out why that was and what has become of the watch.'

'Another thing strikes me,' said Laura. 'It was such a peculiar gift to send to a woman. She couldn't wear the watch; she couldn't even display it to much advantage. A watch isn't like a large, eye-taking clock, or a picture, or a piece of sculpture or furniture, is it?'

'It may have been sent her merely as a keepsake.'

'Perhaps Sir Anthony thought she would sell it. It may have been a way of providing her with money without actually writing a cheque. I wonder how the police came by such a detailed account of the watch?'

'Oh, Mrs Lawrence would have been bound to describe it to them when she complained that she had not received it. Sir Anthony must have sent a covering letter which gave a complete description of the gift.'

'I suppose so. What do we do next?'

'We arrange to interview some of the various parties who have already been interrogated by the police. I have no doubt that the High Mistress has arranged for her porters to be represented by a reputable solicitor, but I will make sure that this has been done. If necessary, I will do it myself. I am sure that the police have not sufficient evidence to charge the men either with theft or with murder, but if they believe they *can* make out a case against them we must see to it that their solicitor manages to get them remanded on bail. The police, I think, would agree to this, since it would give them more time in which to make further enquiries. It would not surprise me, on the other hand, if the magistrates decided that there was no case to answer, or even if the police dropped the charge. They must know, by this time, that they are on unsafe ground.'

Dame Beatrice began her enquiries with a visit to Mrs Lawrence's landlady, who proved co-operative and eager to help.

'For to believe as poor Mr Oates or Tom Wagstaffe did anything so wicked as stealing and murder, I simply could not bring myself,' she said. 'I've known them both from boyhood up, and it isn't in them to act so sinful.'

It transpired, during the course of the interview, that she had not cared overmuch for Mrs Lawrence.

'You'd have thought she was one of the dons, the way she went on. Very high and mighty she was, and with none of their quiet, ladylike ways. Nose in air, that was her. Not that she tried it on with me. I knew her parents when they kept a little bread and bun shop on the Wisden road, and her husband not what I would call a don, neither, he being only a lecturer at a college somewhere up north. Of course I only met him the once and I can't say he struck me as much of a gentleman, if you know what I mean.'

'Oh, really? And when did you meet him?'

'As I told the police when they asked me, it would have been just about this time two years ago, and I never saw him before or since.'

'Did Mrs Lawrence live here during vacations?'

'Easter and Christmas she did, and went into College most days. Sometimes it was to get on with some work and sometimes it was to develop her photographs. She had permission to photograph the university buildings and all that, you see, both inside and out. She was doing it for the Warden of Wayneflete College, she told me, because he was writing a book. That's how she got permissions which would not have been given to an outsider.'

'Apart from that one visit from her husband, did she have other callers?'

'Not gentlemen callers, although I would have had no objection, seeing she was a married woman. There was her brother, of course, but I don't count him, and she used to have three ladies come in one evening a week for a quiet game of bridge, that's all.'

'Apart from her College duties and the darkroom connected with her photography, did she go out very much?'

'Once a week to the cinema and sometimes she'd go to one of her ladyfriends to watch television. I don't allow it here, you see.'

'Oh, really? Why is that?'

'I had to ban it because some of my lodgers used to have it on so loud, and that made others complain. Those that felt they must have it had to go, but I never have empty rooms for long. I've got a reputation for cleanliness and good cooking and a fair rent and no extras, you see. Most of my lodgers are Third Year women students and they've got their work to do of an evening. I don't take the rackety sort.'

'This is all very interesting. What did Mrs Lawrence do during the Long Vacation?'

'She paid me a retaining fee while she was away. That was usually for four weeks. She told me she spent the four weeks with her husband. Of course he may have come here to fetch her. I wouldn't know about that, because I generally go on my own holiday then. I'm a widow with a son living in Skegness, so I go up there to mind the two children while he and his wife go off on their own holiday.'

'So, although you met Mrs Lawrence's husband only once, he may have come here at other times when you were away from home? You mentioned Mrs Lawrence's brother. Did he call here often?'

'Not to say often, and generally on a Sunday, when, of course, she didn't have to go over to College. He used to come about every six weeks. Come on a motor-bike, he did, and they went to the university church, St Mary's that is, in the morning and then she paid me extra for his Sunday lunch and if it was fine they'd walk by the river or in the university parks, or maybe take a punt down the backwater. Very fond of each other they seemed.'

'I suppose you're sure it *was* her brother?' said Laura. The woman looked affronted.

'Of course I'm sure,' she said. 'Mrs Lawrence had photos of him at all ages. There was him as a schoolboy in his tasselled cap, him as a boxer in his shorts and singlet, him in a dinner-jacket with a carnation in his buttonhole and him at her wedding – not as best man, of course, but in the wedding photos standing modest on the outskirts. She told me he gave her away, as their father was dead.'

'I wonder whether the photographs are still in her room?' said Laura.

'Oh, no. The police have got everything like that, and all her letters and things, and of course I've let her rooms, so I couldn't show you over.'

'Have you any idea where the brother lives?'

'No, not really, but it couldn't be all that far away if he could have his breakfast and get here in time for church, could it? I believe she once mentioned Lyndhurst, but I couldn't be sure.'

'How did the police get in touch with him? I understand that he was called upon to identify the body,' said Dame Beatrice.

'I can't tell you anything about that. I suppose they found letters from him among her things. I was on my holiday at the time it all happened, so I really don't know much about it. When I came back, what a shock I got! Her murdered and buried in a nasty sack and the police everywhere, which another of my lodgers had let in and told them which were her rooms. They were locked up, of course, but the police have their ways of opening doors.'

'I suppose she never indicated that she had an enemy?'

'Somebody who would do her a mischief, like murdering her, you mean? Gracious me, no! This is a most respectable house! It was a stranger did it. That College is open to visitors all the Long Vacation. I reckon some nasty man not right in the head followed her into that cellar and that's how it happened. You hear about such goings-on all the time.

'Well, you may hear about such goings-on all the time,' said Laura, as she and Dame Beatrice walked back to the car-park, 'but that brings us back to the question of why any "nasty man" should have buried the body. Lawrence or that brother of hers were the only people who would have wanted to hide it, simply because, once it was found, they would be suspected. It's just the porters' rotten luck about that parcel. Well, what happens now?'

'Another interview with the Chief Constable. The Superintendent may have sent in another report by this time and I should like to know what it is.'

'Going to pull your rank?'

'That is a most unseemly question.'

'So you will, if he turns sticky, but he won't. That's the value of having met people socially. Makes it very difficult for them to go all haughty and stand-offish when you ask them for a load of the dirt.'

'Your intelligence is matched only by the elegance of your conversation,' said Dame Beatrice, cackling.

'What about the wild originality of my countenance?' retorted Laura. 'Let's see; we turn left out of this car-park, don't we? Devil take these one-way streets!'

They stopped at a call-box and Dame Beatrice rang up. The Chief Constable was at home and would be glad to see them. When they arrived they found that he had a police inspector with him.

'The Super has been taken off the rather weak case involving the College porters,' he said, 'to deal with a bank break-in.'

'A bank robbery is a much more important matter than a mere murder, of course,' said Dame Beatrice. 'I believe the two men have been remanded on bail. The case against them is hardly strong enough for them to be in custody.'

'There's the matter of them having a key to the cellar and the fact that the parcel containing a valuable watch has not turned up,' said the inspector, a young man with a red face and a pugnacious jaw. 'We need to keep the tabs on them.'

'Ah, yes, these keys to the cellar,' said Dame Beatrice. 'Has Mrs Lawrence's own key been found?'

'Yes, ma'am, it was on the body. Proves it was one of the porters, seems to me. All our enquiries show that they were the only people, except Mrs Lawrence herself, who had access. Not even the High Mistress had a key. They only had Mrs Lawrence's key cut so's she could use part of the cellar as a dark-room. The fellow who did it must have used his own key, else why was *her* own key still on the body?'

'But surely the murderer could have returned the key to the body before he buried her, could he not?'

'Well, I suppose he *could*, ma'am, but why should he? We don't believe her own key had anything to do with it. I mean, how could any stranger have been able to follow her into the cellar without being spotted? That's why I plump for one of the porters. How could anybody else have got in?'

'Quite easily, I imagine. I don't suppose she locked the door of her darkroom while she was inside it.'

'That gate is in the porter's line of vision all the time, though ma'am.'

'All the time except when his vision is directed elsewhere. A porter's lodge is a place of comings and goings, Inspector. The porter's attention must often be claimed and therefore distracted. Moreover, the murder, it seems, must have taken place at the beginning of the Long Vacation. Well, during the Long Vacation, visitors are freely admitted to the College grounds. There would be no embargo on a quietly behaved, apparently respectable person gaining entrance to Bessie's Quad when he or she knew that Mrs Lawrence was in her cellar darkroom. By watching for an opportunity and then descending into the depths while the porter's attention was elsewhere. . .'

'She'd have heard the murderer and screamed out, ma'am, and if the porter on duty was innocent of the crime, he'd have heard her and come down the cellar steps to investigate.'

'Have you stationed a woman constable in the cellar and instructed her to scream, so that you could find out whether that scream could be heard in the porter's lodge?'

'No, ma'am,' replied the inspector, assuming a wooden expression. 'We didn't think it necessary.'

'You preferred to suspect the porters and leave it at that?'

'Look, we're *certain* one of 'em did it, ma'am. Our job is to find out which one, that's all.'

'It may be "all" from the police point of view. It certainly is not "all" from mine. However, I doubt whether any scream emanated from the victim. The attack would have been sudden and the killing mercifully swift. It is not the easiest thing in the world, in any case, to scream loudly enough to attract attention when one's head is pulled violently backward and the assailant's knee, most probably, is in the small of one's back. Besides, absorbed in her task, the victim may not even have heard her assailant come down the cellar steps.'

'Very well, ma'am. You don't need to labour the point. Perhaps we *haven't* looked quite far enough. When we found her husband had an unbreakable alibi, you see, there was nobody left but the porters and we knew she'd had some bitter words with *them* because of the missing parcel.'

'I will ask you another question, Inspector, if I may.'

He looked resigned; then, to his credit, he grinned.

'Don't mind me, ma'am,' he said.

'Well, have the police asked themselves why the murderer removed the body from the cellar and interred it in the cloister garth?'

'Why, that's an easy one, ma'am. He couldn't just leave it in the cellar. I reckon it had begun to niff a bit by the time he moved it.'

'Yes, that is true, but, you know, Inspector, the only time the porters needed to go into that cellar seems to have been when the deck-chairs had to be brought out for the High Mistress's annual garden-party. If one of the porters was the murderer, would he not have removed the body long before that? – or are you assuming that both porters are guilty?'

'We still don't know what happened to that parcel, ma'am.'

'And if both are guilty, why move the body at all? Nobody used the cellar except themselves and Mrs Lawrence. What is important, as I have said before – but it will bear repetition – is that the parcel which disappeared was never proved to have been delivered at the porters' lodge at all. Besides, it would be interesting to know why it was not sent to the victim's lodgings. One would have thought that a gift such as a valuable watch would have been sent straight there rather than to the College.'

'Yes, indeed, ma'am, but the donor, the old gentleman who sent the watch, is gone where he can't be questioned.'

'Unfortunately that is so. You have questioned his servants, of course?'

'Yes, ma'am, but they recollect little of the matter, except that, if such a parcel was sent, none of them was told to get it registered.'

'What about Mr Lawrence, the husband, Sir Anthony's heir?'

'He reckons to know nothing about the watch and, as you will have been told, we've checked his alibi for the time the doctors think the murder took place and it stands up, there's no doubt about that. He'd come back from Norfolk and was with the old gentleman when he died and then went back to his digs up north, where his landlady swears he stayed put until well after the murder.'

'Alibis are like promises and pie-crust,' said Laura, when they had parted from the inspector. 'We ought to get on to that rascally College scout and turn him inside out about that meeting between Lawrence and Coralie St Malo.'

'If it *was* Coralie St Malo whom he met in that public house,' said Dame Beatrice suddenly. 'Have you ever visited Blackpool?'

'No. My education has been faulty, I'm afraid.'

'A matter which can readily be adjusted. Let us set out tomorrow for the famous resort.'

'Then we had better set out this afternoon for the Stone House to collect a few necessities and I'd better ring up and engage a couple of rooms in Blackpool. Have you a favourite hotel?'

'No, I have never been to Blackpool. My education has been as deficient as your own.'

'The hotels may be full in a place like that at this time of year.'

'That we can soon find out when we get home. We have a guide to hotels and the telephone is at our disposal.'

'And we'd better stay the night at a half-way house; not that I can't manage the distance in one day, but. . .'

'Yes, a two-day journey will be more enjoyable in every way.'

Laura, however was fated not to make the journey to Blackpool. A telephone message to the Stone House informed her that measles had broken out at her daughter's boarding school and that all pupils who were not affected were being sent home and should be met at Waterloo railway station.

Before they left the inspector, Dame Beatrice had obtained from him the name of the concert party which enjoyed Coralie St Malo's services and Dame Beatrice's official card sent in at the morning rehearsal brought a beaming Coralie round to the hotel for lunch.

She was somewhat of a surprise. She was a big woman, quietly dressed, and her make-up was discreet; also, although she spoke in a rather strident, self-assertive voice, her manners would have passed muster anywhere. She appeared to be about thirty years old and she gave an impression of toughness and natural self-confidence. She refused a cocktail and drank very little wine with her meal. They took this at twelve-thirty so that she could get back in good time for the afternoon performance.

'That heel?' she said, when Dame Beatrice introduced Lawrence's name. 'Yes, I met him and we had a drink together. He wanted to re-marry me, but I thought, "Once bitten, twice shy". He said he was coming into a lot of money and couldn't we try to make a go of it again.'

'Re-marry?' asked Dame Beatrice.

'Yes, of all the impudence.'

'You mean that you had been divorced?'

'I'll say! I divorced him at the end of the time allowed for desertion. The suit was undefended. That's why you won't have heard of it, I expect.'

'You know, of course, that he had married a Miss Caret?'

'Told me his divorce from her was pending. Instead, he cut her throat.'

'There is surely no evidence of that?'

'Who needs evidence? You've only got to know him. *My* belief is he did in that poor old gentleman, Sir Anthony, too, who was always so good to him.'

'Oh, you knew Sir Anthony, did you?'

'Of course not. Thaddy – he didn't like me shortening his name, but how can you be expected to call anybody Thaddeus? – it wasn't his real name, anyway. Well, Thaddy wouldn't ever let me meet Sir Anthony. Kept me dark because I was common, you see. Thought perhaps he wouldn't get Sir Anthony's money if the old gentleman found out he'd married somebody on the concert-party stage and, like a fool, I played along with it and let him go off up north where he said he'd send for me when he'd saved enough to put down on a little house. Well, of course, *that* never came off, so when the time was up I divorced him for desertion and irretrievable breakdown, as they call it, but I didn't know that in the meantime he'd taken up with this Caret girl. I found that out later.'

'So his marriage to Miss Caret might have been bigamous if it took place before you divorced him?'

'I suppose so. I wished her joy of him when I found out, which wasn't until after my divorce, and much joy she's had, poor girl, with her throat cut and buried in a nasty, dirty sack!'

'I am interested in your opinion that Lawrence is a murderer. May I ask what may seem to be an impertinent and very personal question, Miss St Malo?' said Dame Beatrice. Coralie looked anxious and, for the first time during the interview, her self-confidence seemed to falter.

'I don't take offence where there's no call for it,' she said, twisting her hands together.

'Thank you. We – the police and I – were told that after the meeting at the public house near Bicester you invited Mr Lawrence to your lodgings, where he stayed for about an hour.'

'He drove me home from the Bicester pub, same as he drove me out there, but I never asked him in and he never came in. Who told you he did?' Her tone was sharper than before.

'One of the scouts at Wayneflete College. At least, he is no longer in service there. He resigned because of an accusation made against him by Mr Lawrence.'

'Oh, Alf Bird! He's a snout and a liar. Everybody knows that. Never happy unless he's got hold of some tit-bit of muck about somebody. He's the original Little-Bird-Told-Me. Thaddy took me up to my front door, took my key like the gentleman he always pretended to be, let me in and then handed back the key and drove off. Bird was just spreading dirt, as usual.'

'Could be true, I suppose,' said Laura, when Dame Beatrice, brought back to Stone House by her chauffeur George, had given an account of the interview. 'Shall you see this man Bird?'

'At this stage it would be useless. He will repeat his story, whether it is true or not. Miss St Malo herself may be lying. Some of the time, in fact, I am sure she was. The next thing, as I see it, is to find that watch. Even if one of the porters did steal it

– a matter difficult of credence in the case of men who held a position of such trust – it cannot still be in the possession of either Oates or Wagstaffe.'

'No. I imagine their hut and their homes have had a pretty fair going-over by the police, and if either of them had sold or popped the watch locally, that would have come out long before this. Are you proposing to go and look for the watch yourself?'

'No,' replied Dame Beatrice, pretending to take the question seriously. 'That would be beyond my scope, I fear. I shall suggest to the Chief Constable that he put it to the inspector that another attempt be made to extract information from old Sir Anthony's servants. It would not surprise me to learn that the watch was never posted at all, but was stolen from Sir Anthony's own house.'

'By Lawrence?'

'According to Ferdinand's report of his conversations with the Warden of Wayneflete College, it would be quite in keeping with Lawrence's reputation. But, to turn to a pleasanter subject, what have you done with my rusticated god-daughter? I expected and hoped to find her here.'

'Sorry, but I wasn't sure how much we'd be here ourselves while this business was still going on, so as it is so near her school summer holiday I've shipped her up to my brother and his wife in Scotland. She was due to go there in a few days' time, anyway.'

'I am sorry to have missed her, but perhaps she is safer out of the way.'

'*Safer?*'

'I do not like this particular murder.'

'I see. You mean we don't need to offer hostages to fortune and all that. It hadn't occurred to me that the murderer might know that we are interesting ourselves in his affairs.'

CHAPTER 10

Afraid of honest men with honest minds.
Afraid, even, of an old woman like me.

'That watch has turned up again, so the inspector informs me,' said the Chief Constable, when Dame Beatrice telephoned him again after her return to the Stone House. 'You've been to Blackpool, have you? Any news?'

'A little, but, so far as the College porters are concerned, perhaps yours is better worthwhile. Could you spare the time to come over and have a chat? I should like very much to hear about the watch.'

'And I should like a detailed account of your visit to Blackpool. You gave me an outline, so perhaps you would be good enough to fill it in?'

'Most willingly. May we expect you to lunch tomorrow?'

'Could it be the following day? The inspector is planning an identity parade, putting both porters in it. It will take a bit of arranging because for obvious reasons he doesn't want to call upon local people to join in. Following the message which you telephoned on your way home – from Preston, I think you said – he's putting Lawrence in the parade, too, I believe – not that I can see much point in it – the parade, I mean.'

'Where is Lawrence now?'

'Still in Sir Anthony's old house. He owns it, of course, and, although it is on the market, it has not been sold yet.'

'Can the inspector insist that he appear in a parade?'

'Oh, well, I suppose that so long as he has nothing to hide, there is no reason why he should refuse to appear. A police car will be sent to bring him here and take him home afterwards. If he has a guilty conscience he will hardly *dare* to refuse the inspector's request. I have had a talk with the inspector and he has suggested that if Lawrence seems reluctant to appear in the identity parade, he should tell him that the man dragging the sack was seen and that it is necessary for him to prove that he was not that man. I'm dubious about the ethics of this, but it's the inspector's case now. I could wish we hadn't had to divert Nicholl to this bank robbery.'

'As I am certain that Lawrence *was* that man, the procedure does not affront me as it might do under other circumstances,' said Dame Beatrice, with an eldritch cackle which disconcerted her hearer at the other end of the line.

When the Chief Constable arrived he was able to report that the Mrs Lawrence case, as he called the murder of the second wife, had shown some interesting developments.

'We photographed a similar sort of watch by permission of the horological section of the University Museum,' he said, 'and got the BBC and ITV to put it out on all networks.'

'Not merely in case of its having been stolen, I assume,' said Dame Beatrice.

'Oh, no. We told them it was connected with a murder enquiry.'

'And you obtained a result?'

'Yes. An antique dealer in London rang us and said that he had purchased such a watch and gave us the date of the sale. It fitted well enough and it also fitted with the story told by the two porters when they were brought before the magistrates. Those, as you know, released them on bail while we continued our enquiries into the murder, for that, of course, far more than the theft of the watch, was the point of interest.'

'And the porters' reaction?'

'They repeated what they had already told the magistrates: that they knew nothing about the watch. At last we believe them.'

'What makes you believe their story now, whereas previously you doubted it?'

'The identity parade. The antique dealer came along and scanned the ranks. He had, at our request, brought his woman assistant with him. The inspector had produced seven men and five women, let Lawrence and the two porters stand anywhere they liked in the line and then had in the dealer and, after him, his assistant. When the dealer had made his pick he was not allowed to meet his assistant until she, too, had made her choice. Do you want to make a guess, Dame Beatrice?'

'I would not, for the world, anticipate the *dénouement*.'

'I see that you *have* made a guess. Yes, without hesitation, each picked out Lawrence. He won't admit it, but we rather think he obtained the watch when, instead of entering Coralie St Malo's lodgings that evening, he went to those of his wife. Her landlady did not see him because she was already on holiday. We asked him how he had come by the watch. He said, "The watch? Good Lord! I thought you were sorting out my wife's murderer! You won't get the tabs on me for that! My dear old friend Sir Anthony gave me the watch, but it was much too ornate for me to wear. I much prefer a wristwatch, anyway. I was going on holiday with Sir Anthony the next day, so I sold the thing to get some holiday money, as I was a bit short. I didn't tell the old boy what I'd done. I let him think my wife was minding the watch for me, as I thought he would be hurt to think I'd sold it." Lawrence is certainly a cool customer, Dame Beatrice, and no mistake.'

'I suppose he swiped the watch,' said Laura. 'What a specimen! Still, it lets out the porters, which is what the High Mistress wanted. I suppose you can't arrest Lawrence for theft and so hold on to him until you can prove he's a murderer?'

'We can't disprove his story about the watch, Mrs Gavin. The servant at Mrs Lawrence's digs says that the lodgers always take in the post, so she has no knowledge of any parcels. In any case, to accuse a man of stealing from his own wife is a tricky business under any circumstances; impossible when she isn't even alive to confirm or deny his account of the matter.'

'I always thought that the theft, if it *was* a theft, took place at Sir Anthony's own house,' said Dame Beatrice, 'but I also think that Mrs Lawrence's accusation against the porters was made, however wrongheadedly, in good faith. Sir Anthony's covering letter describing the watch has not been found among her effects, I suppose?'

'No. We looked – the inspector looked – most carefully at all her papers and correspondence.'

'I have no doubt the letter was sent, or she could hardly have described the watch so exactly. However, one good thing has come out of all this, as Laura pointed out.'

'Oh, yes, the porters are completely exonerated, so now we can turn all our attention to the murder. What impression did you get of the St Malo girl?'

'Not an impression of a girl, but of a mature, tough, self-reliant young woman. According to her account, the quarrel with Lawrence at the Bicester public house was soon resolved. He appears to have planned to divorce the second Mrs Lawrence and to re-unite himself in matrimony with Coralie.'

'I see. Could that constitute a motive for the murder?'

'I hardly think so, for, if Miss St Malo is to be believed, she would have nothing to do with the proposition, so I do not think the question of divorce, whether the second Mrs Lawrence would have agreed to it or not, would have come up.'

'But you still think Lawrence is our murderer?'

'Failing any other candidates, I really think he must be. There is only one doubt in my mind.'

'I know. He's a devious, cowardly devil, as I read him, but not the type to go for the rough stuff.'

'Exactly. He brought about old Sir Anthony's death, I believe, but by a method which can hardly be held against him, since there is no proof that he did not do his best (as he saw it) for the old gentleman in what turned out to be a fatal illness.'

'That is true. We shall never get anywhere on those lines.'

'But if Mrs Lawrence had evidence that Lawrence had knowledge that a sudden shock would kill the old gentleman, especially if medical aid was not forthcoming as soon as the symptoms of a serious condition appeared. . .'

'But we can never prove that Mrs Lawrence did have any such knowledge.'

'And, of course, Coralie St Malo may have been lying when she told me that she had refused Lawrence's offer of re-marriage. After all, he is now a very wealthy man.'

'And you summed her up as a bit of a gold-digger, did you?'

'No, but certainly not the reverse. She struck me as a woman who (to repeat a vulgarism) would know on which side the bread was buttered.'

'Well, the inspector will just have to press on with his enquiries. But to return to a point we agreed on a little earlier; Lawrence doesn't strike either of us as the type who would drag a woman's head back and slit her throat.'

'Quite. What is entirely out of character is unlikely to be the truth. On the other hand, Lawrence could still have been the prowler who buried the body. Another thing is that he has what seems to be a complete alibi for the time the doctors agree that the murder was committed, even allowing for the limits they suggest. He was either with Sir Anthony in Norfolk and still with him when the old man died, or in his College lodgings. His landlady is prepared to swear that once he had returned to his northern digs, he did not leave them again until well after the time-limit which the doctors say is the latest date on which the murder could have been committed.'

'It looks as though we'd better lean pretty heavily on the St Malo woman, then, although throat-slitting hardly seems a woman's crime.'

'Unless in her formative years she had seen pigs killed,' said Dame Beatrice, 'and in her part of the country that would hardly have been an uncommon occurrence, I dare say.'

'Well, now that the High Mistress's mission is accomplished without any help from us – for the porters are well and truly cleared – we may take up the even tenor of our way again and you can go off to visit Eiladh and her aunt and uncle in Scotland as soon as ever you like,' said Dame Beatrice.

'Well – ' said Laura dubiously.

'You had better take my car instead of your own. I shall not be needing it while George has his holiday.'

'Well – '

'No, no. Your plans were made weeks ago and now that we can leave everything connected with the murder in the hands of the police, there is no reason whatever for changing the arrangements. Now that the porters are cleared, our interest in the murder of Mrs Lawrence is no longer anything but academic.'

She herself was not at all convinced of this, although the thought that she might be in danger of receiving a visit from Lawrence did not cross her mind. She did realise, later on, that it might have been as well if she had had the opportunity to familiarise herself with Lawrence's features and general appearance, but there had been no opportunity offered her for this, neither had she sought one.

When, therefore, he rang her front-door bell a day or two after Laura and the chauffeur had left the Stone House and her elderly French housekeeper came to the library to announce that a Mr Randolph had called, Dame Beatrice merely asked:

'What does he want? I'm busy.'

'He wish to consult madame.'

'What about?'

'*Le psychologie*. Disturbances of ze mind. *Les hallucinations*, madame.'

'Really?' said Dame Beatrice. 'Well, tell him that I am no longer in private practice and that, in any case, I see no one without either a personal invitation or by appointment.'

'*Bien, madame*.' Celestine withdrew, but before Dame Beatrice could settle down to work again on a paper she was writing for a learned journal, Celestine was back, this time in a state of high indignation.

'Imagine, madame! This assassin of whom I speak to you! He refuses to leave. He has tried to bribe me, madame! He offers me a *pourboire* – and a very small one, at that! – to show him in to you. It is insupportable!'

'I hope you and Henri, between you, will make it clear to him that I can be of no assistance to him.'

'He is *indécrottable*, that one, madame. Henri have to hold him *en mer* –'

'At bay, not "at sea".'

'Bay *is* sea, no? *Eh, bien*, Henri have to hold him *at bay* with a big knife, so he does not force his way into the presence of madame.'

'He appears to be a man of obstinate resolution. You had better show him in here if he is being threatened with a knife.'

'Madame will receive this *parvenu*?'

The man who entered was tall and lean. He was clean-shaven, dark-haired and looked sardonic and ill-humoured. He bowed and took the seat Dame Beatrice offered him.

'Perhaps I should have made an appointment?' he said.

'It would have been of no use,' Dame Beatrice replied. 'I am no longer in private practice.'

'Oh, I had hoped – your son told me –'

'My son?'

'Sir Ferdinand Lestrange. When he knew I wanted to buy a New Forest property, he told me that you and I were to be near neighbours. I shall be moving to a property just outside the town of Chardle.'

'That is not very near the village here.'

'A mere matter of twenty miles. Nothing in a fast car.'

'My son is not usually anxious to extend my circle of acquaintances. He believes that I am capable of doing that for myself.'

'Oh, but people living in the same neighbourhood should be prepared to socialise, surely?'

'I am afraid that my interests lie elsewhere.'

'Oh, now, now!' cried the visitor, wagging a playful finger. 'We are all members one of another, we're told. Doesn't John Donne add that. . .'

'My dear young man,' said Dame Beatrice, 'you told my servant that you had come to consult me professionally.'

'Oh, yes, of course, that is so.'

'I sent a message to say that I am no longer in private practice. Even if I were, you would have had to consult me in London, not here. This is my private residence and I do not welcome –' she eyed him straightly '– gatecrashers.'

'Well, really!'

'Also I happen to be very busy at this particular time, as, no doubt, you can see for yourself.'

'Oh, well!' He rose and stood looking down on her. His hat was in one hand, a pair of driving-gloves in the other. The knuckles of both hands, she noticed, were white.

'I can see that you are under considerable strain,' she said. 'You would do well, perhaps, to consult a doctor.'

'But not you? I could make it any time which suited you.'

'I am sorry. And now, if you don't mind –' She indicated the books and papers on her desk.

'Oh, but, hang it all! Well, look here, if you won't have me as your patient, whom do you suggest I should go to?'

'Professor Jericho is a very good man,' said Dame Beatrice coolly. She rang the bell.

'Go to – ? Here, I say! I *did* expect to get at least a courteous hearing! I came here to –'

'Celestine,' said Dame Beatrice, 'show Mr Lawrence out.'

The Frenchwoman showed no surprise at the change in the visitor's name, but having closed the front door behind him she returned unbidden to her mistress.

'He asks me, that one, whether you are alone in the house except for your servants, madame.'

'Oh? What did you tell him?'

'Big lies.'

'Good. That man, if I mistake not, is a murderer.'

'*Ciel*! *En verité*, madame? I go round with Henri tonight to be sure he lock and double-lock all doors. I am glad it is also windows which can be locked since the attack on the life of madame last year.'

'Yes, Mrs Gavin insisted on the window fastenings. That will be all.'

'I could wish,' muttered Celestine, as she went to the door, 'that the good Georges and Madame Gavin were here to protect madame.'

'Don't worry,' said Dame Beatrice, whose ears were keen, 'I shall now load my little revolver and keep it handy, but I think our visitor, having proved my mettle, is most unlikely to return.'

She rang up the Chief Constable and told him of the visit.

'What did he come for? What was his object, do you suppose?' he asked.

'I think he had been in touch with Miss St Malo and took fright at what she told him of my visit to her. He has much on his conscience and for that reason he probably takes fright very easily. I think he decided to come along and take a look at me and my establishment just to see how the land lay. He found it harsh and inhospitable.'

'Well, apart from the telephone directory – you public figures ought never to allow your names and addresses to appear in that, you know – I suppose it's easy enough to find out from *Who's Who* where you live and all about you. Are you going to ask for police protection?'

'Because a man calls on me and stays less than ten minutes?'

'You say he gave a false name? How did you know it was Lawrence?'

'I did not know. He answered to a description my son once gave me of Lawrence. Besides, like that son, I have a suspicious mind and I am always wary of strangers, especially of strangers who try to bribe my servants. For all these reasons, I guessed who my visitor was.'

'Do you think you were wise to let him know you had recognised him?'

'I did it deliberately. It will be interesting to find out how he reacts, if he reacts at all.'

'It may be interesting, but it won't be very pleasant if he cuts your throat,' said the Chief Constable grimly. 'Do, at least, let your village bobby know that a suspicious-looking stranger has called on you. If nothing more than your visit to Coralie St Malo has put wind up him, he must be in a rare old funk, and so am I, knowing that he's on the loose in your neighbourhood.'

'Very well. If it will ease your mind I will drive into Brockenhurst and acquaint the police with my fears.'

'Your *fears*? That will be the day!' said the Chief Constable.

Dame Beatrice had been placed under police protection once or twice before, although she herself had never asked for it; the safety measure had been taken either by Laura Gavin or by Sir Ferdinand Lestrange on his mother's behalf. On this occasion, however, she kept her word to the Chief Constable and was assured: 'We always keep an eye on your place, ma'am, the nature of your occupation being what it is with the Home Office. Some of your murderers have plenty of friends outside.' So, having done what she could, Dame Beatrice dismissed Lawrence from her mind.

Some days went by, the little pile of manuscript (to be typed when Laura returned) grew a little bulkier, correspondence was dealt with and, for a change of occupation, Dame Beatrice paid visits to her rose-garden to snip off the dead blooms, and so time passed.

The Chief Constable wrote to tell her that Chief Superintendent Nicholl was back in charge of the Lawrence case, but, so far, had no progress to report, all further attempts to break Lawrence's alibi having failed. As for Coralie St Malo and Mrs Lawrence's brother, Bill Caret, all enquiries concerning them came to nothing.

So matters stood and so they remained. Laura and George returned to the Stone House and at the end of September the university's Long Vacation ended. Routine of a pleasant, peaceful kind was re-established at the Stone House and the only surprise, if such it could be called, was that Lawrence had not returned to resume his northern university lectureship, but had resigned it on the grounds that he was now 'a man of property' domiciled in the south.

CHAPTER 11

Off he goes, as nimble as a tadpole,
Only more bullet-headed.

Laura, fortified by her holiday, settled down readily and happily again at the Stone House, her days filled with interesting and pleasurable occupations; but she needed very little sleep and during the wakeful watches of the night she turned her thoughts time and again to the murder of the second Mrs Lawrence and to Lawrence's abortive visit to Dame Beatrice.

One morning, when Dame Beatrice's manuscript was typed and had been posted, she said at breakfast:

'There must be some way of breaking Lawrence's alibi.'

'Unless he committed the murder, he does not need an alibi, dear child.'

'I don't like that visit he paid you when George and I were both away. I think he's our murderer all right and if only that alibi isn't an alibi at all, the police ought to be in a position to charge him.'

'I believe him to be the murderer of old Sir Anthony, and I think Mrs Lawrence had some evidence of this. I believe he may have wanted to kill her, and I believe he was the prowler with the sack who buried her, but I do not believe he carried out the actual murder. I believe he was capable of *poisoning* Mrs Lawrence; I do *not* believe he was capable of cutting her throat. Now that I have met him I believe it even less than I did when I had his early history from Ferdinand, who got it from the Warden of Wayneflete.'

'All the same, I'd like to have a go at that landlady of his, to see whether I couldn't break her down.'

'You are hardly likely to succeed where the police have failed.'

'Oh, I don't know. Woman to woman might dig up some information which wouldn't have been given to a male copper, don't you think?'

'I hardly know what reason you could give for calling upon and questioning her.'

'I bet I could think of something. Anyway, I won't attempt to go up there so soon after Lawrence's visit to you. I think that at present the more able-bodied citizens we have in and about this house, the better prepared we shall be if he has any rough stuff in mind.'

'He hardly gave that impression,' said Dame Beatrice. The next news came from the Warden of Wayneflete himself. It was relayed to the Stone House by Sir Ferdinand. He telephoned his mother to ask whether he might come to dinner and stay the night, as he was defending in Winchester on the following day.

'I shall put up at the Domus after that, while the case lasts, to be handy for the court,' he said, 'but it does seem a good opportunity to come and see you, if you can have me.'

The news he brought was interesting and, in Dame Beatrice's opinion, significant. Sir Ferdinand himself regarded it as having a somewhat humorous aspect.

'These smart-Alecs,' he said, 'they *will* do it, you know, even if their solicitors advise against it. What they expect to get out of it, I don't know.'

'Of what do we speak, my dear boy?'

'This insane decision to go for jury trial instead of biting the bullet on what the magistrates dish out. This lunatic would have got off with four months at the most if he'd opted for summary conviction. As it is, the judge has given him two years.'

'And his offence?'

'Drunken driving.'

'And who is this rash speculator? I gather it is somebody we know.'

'Our friend Thaddeus E. Lawrence, none other. Even going before a judge he might have got off more lightly except that, before sentence was passed, he decided to turn cheeky and called the judge "you misbegotten bastard by Colonel Blimp out of the

Band of Hope". That cooked his goose, of course, and to clinch it he biffed his warder.'

'I wish I'd heard him say it,' remarked Laura. 'I wouldn't have believed he was such a sportsman. So he's behind bars for two years, is he? Less, if he behaves himself, of course.'

'I fancy there is method in his madness,' said Dame Beatrice. 'At least in prison he will be safe from his enemies and from the hand of all that hate him.'

Laura looked at her employer with astonishment.

'You mean he feels we're on his track and may be getting warm?' she asked. 'I didn't think that, up to the present, we'd managed to get anything on him which would stick. You must have said something which frightened him pretty badly when he called on you.'

'Oh, it is not I and it is not the police he fears. My reading of the matter is that he is being pursued by an avenger and that he sees prison as his only chance to put off an evil day. There is a porpoise close behind him, or so I think. He must be in fear of his life to have chosen prison as his only safe hiding-place.'

'Elucidate, mother,' said Ferdinand.

'Well, as I have been known to suggest, the relationship between brothers and sisters is a strange one.'

'And Mrs Lawrence had a brother,' said Laura. 'Yes, but, according to the folklore of the Border ballads, brothers don't kill their sisters' husbands, only their boyfriends or the sisters themselves. See "Clerk Saunders" and "The Cruel Brother".'

'Six of the seven brothers were unwilling to murder Clerk Saunders,' Dame Beatrice pointed out, 'and, in the case of the cruel brother, we are given to understand that it was pique which caused him to stab his sister to death. He had not been consulted about the marriage or asked for his consent to it. We are told of the prospective bridegroom:

> He has sought her from her father, the King
> And sae did he her mither, the Queen.
> He has sought her from her sister Anne;
> But he has forgot her brother John.

With good reason, perhaps.'

'Knowing that John would have refused his consent and that might have ditched the marriage, you mean? Do you think Mrs L's brother objected to her marriage?'

'At any rate, he appears to have had an affectionate regard for her. You will remember our hearing of frequent visits, walks and boating. If he thinks Lawrence had any hand in her death he well might meditate upon revenge.'

'And that's what you think Lawrence knows?'

'According to what Ferdinand has just told us, it seems very likely.'

'Yes, he's an offensive little swine in private life, ' said Sir Ferdinand, 'but I would say that his outburst in court was so uncharacteristic that I'm sure my mother is right and that he was determined to get himself jugged.'

'But that could mean the brother knows something against him,' said Laura.

'It cannot be anything he can prove, or surely he would have gone to the police with it,' said Sir Ferdinand. 'Besides, if mother is right – and I'm sure she is – Lawrence fears private vengeance. Actually, I feel pretty sure that he is not the murderer, although he well may be the accessory after the fact. It looks to me as though the actual killing was done by an accomplice who then left Lawrence's flat.'

'How long do you expect your case at Winchester to last? Shall we see you again when it is over? ' Dame Beatrice enquired.

'Yes, thanks, mother. The wife of my bosom has taken her own mother to Madeira for a period of convalescence, so I'd like to drop by again, if I may. By my reading, my case should last the best part of a week or maybe longer. It's a little matter of theft followed by death. My client stole from a warehouse and, interrupted by the night watchman, hit the latter and killed him. The prosecution will quote R. v. Jones, of course, when Jones was convicted of murdering a store-manager and had his appeal dismissed. There was a reasonable doubt, in my opinion, whether Jones intended to do more than disable the manager of the store which he had burgled, but I doubt whether, in the case I am defending, I can do any better than a verdict of manslaughter, although I shall do my best to "soften the evidence", as that rascal Peachum would say.'

'The murder of Mrs Lawrence could hardly boil down to a charge of manslaughter,' said Laura. 'It was deliberate murder, premeditated, workmanlike and callous.'

Chief Superintendent Nicholl looked dubious.

'But if it's a proper question, Mrs Gavin,' he said, 'what do you expect to get at his landlady's?'

'I'm hoping to break down his alibi for the week Mrs Lawrence was murdered.'

'Well, I wish you more luck than we've had.'

'Woman to woman, and all that kind of thing, you know. What sort of woman is she?'

'A most respectable old party. Has let rooms to the College for years and never a breath against her. If you don't mind me saying so, Mrs Gavin, ma'am, I think you'll be wasting your time.'

'We'll see. You never know.'

She drove off blithely to the address he had given her, but her visit proved to be as abortive as the superintendent had prophesied. Lawrence's lodgings were in a much larger house than Laura had envisaged. It was a solidly built, three-storey Victorian mansion, well maintained; it had a neat front garden, a polished brass knocker, doorbell and letter-flap, and in answer to her ring the front door was opened by a maid capped and aproned and with a well-scrubbed, fresh-complexioned face. This girl stood politely awaiting the caller's opening remarks.

Laura produced Dame Beatrice's official card with her own name added to it in Dame Beatrice's handwriting.

'I wonder whether I could speak to Mrs Breaston?' she said.

'Come inside, madam, please. I'll go and ask. Would it be about a room? – because I don't believe we have a vacancy.'

'Oh? Has Mr Lawrence's room been re-let, then?' asked Laura, who had not foreseen such a useful opening to her visit.

'I'll speak to Mrs Breaston, madam, if you'll kindly take a seat.'

There was a small table in the hall with a chair at either end of it. Laura sat down and was not kept waiting. Mrs Breaston reminded Laura of nobody so much as of the enigmatic housekeeper at Manderley. She was a tall ramrod of a woman dressed all in black. She glided like a fictional nun and carried her hands clasped just below her waist. She was decorated with a large cameo brooch and a long gold chain at the end of which Laura could see a gold cross. Her hair was strained into a small bun at the back of her neck and she wafted before her a faint odour of aniseed.

'I have no vacancies,' she said, 'but your card hardly suggests that you need one. The Home Office? Are you connected with the police force? If so, I am going to complain to my Member of Parliament. I really must protest about being badgered in this way.'

'I am not a member of the police force, neither have I any intention of badgering you, Mrs Breaston. Did you know that Mr Lawrence has been sent to prison for dangerous driving?'

'I have no wish to hear Mr Lawrence's name spoken.'

'I suppose he did leave you rather suddenly. Was he up-to-date with his rent?'

'I have no complaints about that. Perhaps we had better go into my sitting-room. The servants are all ears.' She led the way along the hall and opened a door. The room was papered in a gloomy shade of red which (thought Laura) would have been handy for covering up bloodstains. The curtains were red and so was the carpet, and such light as penetrated to the room came in through the slats of a Venetian blind. 'Please be seated,' the landlady continued. 'Now what is your business here?'

'If Mr Lawrence's name is not to be mentioned, I can hardly answer that question.'

'You say Mr Lawrence is in prison?'

'Yes, for drunken driving and for insulting the judge.'

'That astonishes me. I would not have thought he had the courage for either misdemeanour.'

'Did you ever hear him mention a woman named Coralie St Malo?'

'She sounds like an adventuress,' commented Mrs Breaston remaining within the period which she and her sitting-room so ably represented.

'She's on the concert-party stage. At present she is playing in Blackpool.'

'I know of no such person.'

'Did Mr Lawrence have any women visitors while he was with you?'

'He gave extra coaching to one or two of the female students, but one could hardly call them women visitors and, of course, I saw to it that they left at a reasonable hour. Supper here is at nine. They were always out of this house before that. What is more, if only one young woman at a time was involved, I sat in the room while the tutoring was going on. I thought it only right.'

'I see. Had you any idea that Mr Lawrence was not going to renew his tenancy after the end of the summer term?'

'Mr Lawrence was under notice to go.'

'Oh, really?'

'I discovered that he was having improper relations with one of my maids.'

'Oh, dear!'

'Of course that sealed his fate – and hers.'

'I suppose so – yes. You can be certain that he was here . . .'

'As I have already told the police, Mr Lawrence left this house on May twenty-fourth, having no more lectures to deliver, although it was not, strictly speaking, the end of the term, and he returned here, by my permission, in order to collect the rest of his possessions and work out his notice. I have not seen him since and have no wish to set eyes on him again.'

'Well, I don't suppose you will, Mrs Breaston. He has been given a two-year prison sentence. Now, those last nights after his return, he *was* in this house all the time, I suppose?'

'He was.'

'May I ask how you can be so sure?'

'I kept my eye on him every day and my ears open.'

'Can you be certain he did not slip out at night?'

'Yes,' said the landlady grimly, 'that I can. I trusted him so little that I had all his possessions moved into the room next to mine. Since you appear to have official standing, I will show you how I can be certain he did not leave my house. Not that I should have been concerned about *that*. It was his morals *inside* my house which concerned me.'

She led the way majestically from the room and up the well-carpeted stairs. She unlocked a door on the landing.

'This is your bedroom, I take it,' said Laura, looking around.

'That is so.' The landlady traversed the room and opened a door which communicated with it. 'And *this* is where I put Mr Lawrence with the door between us securely bolted on my side of it. You will notice that there is no other method of egress from this room. I always dressed early, tidied my room and then unbolted the communicating door.'

Laura walked over to what had been Lawrence's bedroom window during his last short stay in the house, a stay which, according to the medical evidence, must have covered the period during which the murder of Mrs Lawrence had taken place. There was a sheer drop of more than thirty feet on to a stone courtyard. 'He could have buried the body but not committed the murder,' thought Laura.

'I am sorry, but not surprised, that you had your journey for nothing,' said Dame Beatrice.

'Well, it wasn't quite for nothing, because I've satisfied myself that Lawrence must be in the clear so far as the actual murder of Mrs Lawrence is concerned. We know he went to Wayneflete College, where Sir Ferdinand spoke to him about the money that was embezzled, and Mrs Lawrence certainly wasn't killed while he was there.'

'No. The session at her university was not over, so she certainly would have been missed if she hadn't turned up at Abbesses College during the last few days of term.'

'Then we know that Lawrence spent a week with Sir Anthony in Norfolk. His alibi is clear for that time, too, and also for the five days which followed, for these included all the arrangements for Sir Anthony's funeral and also the funeral itself. Still, according to Miss Runmede's evidence, Lawrence may be covered for his wife's *murder*, but he *isn't* cleared of that business of the sack and the cloister garth. That means he had guilty knowledge of the murder, even if he didn't commit it. For long enough we have been agreed upon that.'

'Coralie St Malo?' said Chief Superintendent Nicholl who, having cleared up his bank robbery, was now pursuing what he thought was a dead end. 'Oh, I don't know about that, Mrs Gavin. We've nothing on her at all. There's no motive and we haven't found the murder weapon. It's buried deep in the river mud, we reckon. Except that it was probably a cut-throat razor, or so Forensic tell us, we know nothing about it, although, of course, we're still making enquiries. If it was a cut-throat razor it must have been somebody's family heirloom. Nobody buys such things nowadays, so there's no point in trying the shops, although, of course, we've had a go.'

'Coralie could have had opportunity, though,' urged Laura. 'She could have been in the neighbourhood at about the time of the murder.'

'She met Lawrence in that pub before the murder was committed, and that's all we know, Mrs Gavin. But we'll keep the tabs on her, of course. All the same, this wasn't a woman's crime.'

'Clytemnestra did in Agamemnon with an axe; Lizzie Borden finished off her parents, ditto; Constance Kent was accused of cutting her little brother's throat, Procne killed and cooked her son. . .'

'All very mythical, Mrs Gavin. Nobody knows whether it was Lizzie Borden or not. As for Constance Kent, there's never been any doubt in my mind that it was the father who cut the child's throat. After all, he'd slept with the nursemaid in the same room as the little boy. It only needed for the kid to wake up and start asking awkward questions. Constance was at the self-sacrificing age and so decided to carry the can. That's my reading of it.' He looked at Dame Beatrice for confirmation of this view. '*You* know all about psychology, ma'am. What's your view about Constance Kent?'

'She may have *wished* her half-brother dead,' said Dame Beatrice, 'and that, in a neurotic adolescent, may have induced a feeling of guilt for which she felt expiation was appropriate.'

'Well, what *about* Coralie St Malo?' persisted Laura. 'According to the description Dame Beatrice gave me, she was big enough and strong enough to have done the deed, yes, and tough enough, too, and probably insanely jealous, into the bargain.'

'We shall be pursuing our enquiries, Mrs Gavin,' said Nicholl, soothingly.

'What do *you* think?' asked Laura, when she and Dame Beatrice were alone again.

'I think Lawrence and Miss St Malo might be well advised to re-marry,' said Dame Beatrice, 'unless Miss St Malo joins a concert party ready and willing to go to South America and stay there.'

'In other words, those of the scoundrel Peachum to the scoundrel Lockit, Lawrence and Coralie are in the position, you think, of having to admit; unless they marry again, "You know we have it in our power to hang each other." And that's about the size of it, so far as culpability is concerned. Coralie did the dirty work and Lawrence buried the body. I suppose it was a case of Macbeth and Lady Macbeth.'

'It was Macbeth who wielded the dagger, if you remember. The play is not an analogy for the murder of Mrs Lawrence.'

'So what?'

'So, between them, Lawrence and Miss St Malo were responsible for Mrs Lawrence's death and burial, but I do not think that will ever be proved.'

As though to confirm this prophecy, the spy who had trailed Coralie and Lawrence to the Bicester road public house was found dead in a ditch "with twenty trenched gashes on his head", the result, the police concluded, of a brawl. His assailants were never brought to book.

PART THREE

Cracks in the Plaster

CHAPTER 12

Training their own minds and the minds of others.
. . . Keenly alert in disputation.

The annual general meeting of the Chardle and district amateur dramatic, operatic and literary society was winding down to its close, or so some of the more restless and impatient members hoped.

The minutes of the last annual general meeting had been read, agreed and signed, reports had been given by the secretary, the treasurer and the entertainments secretary, the balance sheet had been approved, the re-election of the president (who was chairman of the meeting), the secretary and the treasurer, had been confirmed with acclamation (since nobody wanted their jobs), the entertainments' secretary and two members of the committee had resigned and had been replaced, and several attempts on the part of the frivolous-minded and the tedious members (the society was made up in about equal parts of both) to enter into side-issues had been repressed with admirable firmness by the chairman, so at last the final item on the agenda had been reached.

'Any other business?' asked the chairman. He was a florid man of fifty-five with the fleshy, petulant face of an eighteenth-century landowner and somewhat shifty grey eyes. In point of fact, he *was* a landowner of sorts, for he had been a prosperous local builder and had amassed a small fortune before land became too difficult or too expensive to acquire. Having purchased his own plot, however, some years previously, he had disposed of his business, built himself an impressive residence on the outskirts of the town and had become chairman of the local council as well as president of the dramatic and operatic society whose annual general meeting he was now itching to declare closed. He had a masonic dinner to attend that evening and he wanted to get home and change his clothes.

As he uttered the words 'Any other business' he gave a quick and apprehensive half-glance at Clarice Blaine, the new entertainments' secretary. He had known occasions when, under her guidance, 'Any other business' had aroused worse passions, had led to more acrimonious arguments and had wasted more time than any other three items put together.

As though his half-glance had been a challenge, Mrs Blaine responded to it immediately. She was the elder of the two married women present, a plump, self-assertive busybody of forty-five, self-appointed leader of the local Ladies' Guild, terror of the minister whose chapel she attended and the *bête noire* of the dramatic society and especially of its president and chairman, Hamilton Haynings. She, like himself, was on the town council and had managed to project herself on to three of its sub-committees. It was well-known that she was working hard to have Chardle recognised as a borough, and of this borough she intended to be the first mayor.

'Of course there is other business, Hamilton,' she said briskly. 'I'm surprised it was not listed under its title when Cyril sent round the agenda.' She looked accusingly at the handsome secretary. 'There is the Caxton Festival to discuss.'

'I thought your Ladies' Guild had that in hand,' said the treasurer, a meek man named Ernest Farrow, nervously taking off his glasses.

'Oh, the Guild are putting on a pageant, of course,' said Clarice, 'but surely the Dramatic Society ought to perform a Festival play? I *quite* thought members would come to this meeting positively *bursting* with suggestions.'

'We decided upon our next production weeks ago,' said Rodney Crashaw, who had been given the leading part in it. 'We're committed to *Othello*. I've already learnt half my lines. You can't change the play now.'

'Oh, yes, we'll do *Othello*, of course,' said Mrs Blaine, 'but that can come later. It is hardly what I call a *Festival* piece. We need something cheerful.'

'I couldn't agree more!' said Melanie Cardew, who felt that, with her histrionic ability, which, for an amateur, was considerable, she should have been given the part of Desdemona, but who had been fobbed off (as she expressed it) with Bianca, mistress to Cassio, in favour of a younger, prettier Desdemona. 'Of course we must take part in the Festival. What about doing *Blithe Spirit*?' (Mentally she cast herself as Elvira.)

'Not possible,' said a young man who was responsible for the lighting and stage effects. 'The effects for that are a pro. job. We'd never be able to pull off all the ghost stuff and the rest of it. It's out of the question.'

'What about. . .?' began another voice. The chairman rapped on his table.

'Please, *please*!' he said. 'This is not the time. The secretary will convene another meeting if members want to put on a special play for the Caxton Festival. Will someone propose? – Thank you. Seconded? – Thank you. Those in favour of a Festival play? Carried. I declare the meeting closed.' He glanced at his watch and hurriedly gathered up his papers. 'The secretary will convene a special meeting.'

The special meeting took place at the end of a fortnight, during which time there was much private canvassing, especially on the part of the women members, most of whom had a favourite part (the leading one, of course) for which she fancied her talents fitted her. Nobody was anxious to boost a rival's claims, however, and no agreement had been reached. The members, armed with arguments and scripts, assembled in the school classroom which had been booked for the meeting and there was an air of uneasiness mixed with hostility abroad.

The gathering was a smaller one than the annual general meeting. The president, the secretary, the treasurer and Mrs Blaine were present and so were those members who thought they stood any chance of a part in the Festival production. So also were Laura Gavin and another recently joined member, a lecturer in music and drama at the Chardle College of Education. His name was Denbigh and he had been invited – in fact, almost begged – to join the society, and had decided to do so.

Cyril Wincott, the secretary, was a rising young schoolmaster who had set his sights on a lectureship at the College and thought that a friend at court would be an advantage. The treasurer,

Ernest Farrow, was equally anxious to take advantage of Denbigh's membership, but for a different reason. Ever mindful of the society's finances, he thought that perhaps Denbigh could see to it that a rehearsal room at the College would be placed, free of charge, at the disposal of the society in place of the school classroom for meetings and the school hall and stage for rehearsals, where both room and hall had to be rented.

Laura, who was almost as new a member as Denbigh himself, did not anticipate that she would be offered a part. She had come to enjoy the fun when the fighting started and the vested interests began to clash. Denbigh was there because, although he had brought no script, he was prepared with a suggestion if it should be called for.

Clarice Blaine, in her new capacity as entertainments' secretary, made a spirited bid to take charge of the proceedings.

'Well,' she said gaily, 'if everybody will take a seat, we can get on without wasting time. I think Hamilton is ready to open the meeting. There seem to be a good many books and scripts in evidence, so that means plenty of suggestions, I hope, for the Festival play. Of course, the subject matter must not compete with my ideas for the Guild pageant, but I shall be able to put the brake on there, as the Guild plans are almost complete. Now, Hamilton, I think we are all ready to begin.'

'Thank you, Clarice,' said Hamilton Haynings angrily. 'Well, I am open to – I mean, I declare the meeting open for any suggestions. First of all, we have to decide whether we are to do a Festival play at all. Most of you seemed to be in favour, but some may have changed their minds.'

'Of course we're going to do a Festival play,' said Melanie Cardew, that haggard, intense spinster of twenty-nine. She received a chorus of support from the women members. The men were less enthusiastic.

'I thought I'd mentioned at the last meeting that we'd settled on our next production,' said Rodney Crashaw. 'I repeat that we have settled upon *Othello* and that I've already learnt half my lines. Why go back on our arrangements?'

'I never agreed with *Othello*,' said Melanie, still sore that she had not been offered the part of Desdemona, although this was for reasons obvious to everybody except herself.

'Neither did I,' said Stella Walker, a dark-haired, pretty, witless girl of twenty. 'Look what a frost *Hedda Gabler* was! The classics are all very well, I suppose, but you don't want to overdo them just because royalties don't have to be paid.'

'If you had to manage the finances of this society,' began Ernest Farrow.

'Please, *please*!' said the chairman.

'I agree,' said Sybil Gartner, who was studying to become a professional singer. '*Othello* was a mistake. It isn't a play for amateurs, any more than *Hedda*, and *Hedda* was a complete mess. Why can't we do a musical?'

Marigold Tench, who had taken the name part in *Hedda Gabler*, got up and walked out of the room.

'Oh, dear! Now I've put my foot in it, but, honestly, I meant nothing *personal*,' protested Sybil, who was often in rivalry with Marigold both in the interests of Melpomene and Eros. '*Hedda* was a flop. We couldn't fill the hall any one of the three nights and those people who *did* come hadn't a good word to say for the production. Anyway, what *about* a musical? I mean, what's the use of calling ourselves an operatic society if we never get a chance to sing? The last three shows have all been straight plays, so wouldn't it be a good idea...'

'The members know quite well why we can't often do a musical,' said the treasurer desperately. 'It's the expense. We have to hire an orchestra and a conductor. When we did *Rose-Marie* we were in the red for three years. I ought to know. I had the accounts to do. We had to borrow from the bank to pay most of our expenses, and if...'

'Yes,' said the disgruntled Crashaw, a bearded, dark-haired, saturnine man, 'I agree. If Ernest hadn't worked like a beaver to sell the tickets and cut our losses wherever he could, and if I myself – although I hate to remind you – hadn't guaranteed us...'

'Please, *please*!' shouted the chairman, rapping irritably on the teacher's table as a chorus broke out. 'We have no time for these arguments. And,' he added, looking at Crashaw, whose elegantly bearded chin was elevated in purposeful fashion, 'you may recollect that it was also *my* influence which caused the bank to tide us over. We all know what an excellent treasurer Ernest is, and that Rodney is, apart from myself, our most affluent member, but do let us forget all that for the moment and get down to business. I declare the meeting open for suggestions and general discussion. We *must* have order and method.'

'Quite so,' agreed Mrs Blaine. 'I suggest that all who have anything to put forward should occupy the front of the room. I will write up all the suggestions on the blackboard and then we can vote upon them.'

Without waiting for any reply, she took her place at the blackboard, picked up a piece of chalk from a box which was on the teacher's (now the chairman's) table and prepared to do as she had said.

'An excellent suggestion, Clarice,' said the chairman, annoyed at this blatant usurpation of his rights, 'except that I think the meeting had better be left in my hands and that any writing had better be left to the secretary.'

'I still don't see why we can't do *Blithe Spirit*,' said Melanie Cardew, resting her haggard gaze upon the chairman. She was proud of her ravaged looks and thought of herself as a *femme fatale*.

'That's been answered,' said Haynings. 'The effects would be impossible to manage.'

'Only so far. I mean, nobody is going to expect a London production. A lot of *tulle*, or even butter-muslin, could be draped around Elvira and somebody could agitate the backcloth. . .'

Mrs Blaine, refusing to resume her seat, wrote *Blithe Spirit* on the blackboard and, to signify her own opinion of the suggestion, placed a large, almost insolent question mark against it. This started the ball rolling. Suggestions came fast and furious and so did the objections to them.

'*The Importance of Being Ernest*,' said a member.

'Far too elegant and mannered. We'd never pull it off after people have seen Dame Edith and Sir Laurence and all that lot,' said another.

'What about *The Dover Road*?'

'Only six characters, apart from the footmen and chambermaids. Besides, there's no *body* to it. Nothing to get your teeth into.'

'Body? Yes, what about a thriller? Murder always goes down

well,' said a young man.

'A comedy-thriller! *The Cat and the Canary*?' shouted his friend.

'*Night Must Fall*?'

'We'd never pull it off. That's a play for professionals. Where would we find an Emlyn Williams?'

'Why don't we do another pantomime?' asked a large blonde who claimed that before her retirement from it, she had been on the professional stage. 'Aladdin would be nice. I could do the name part, with a bit of song and dance thrown in, and Tad –'

'You shouldn't use pet names in public, Miss Mabelle,' said Othello hastily. 'When we were kids in the States,' he explained unnecessarily to the company at large, 'I was called by my second name, Frederick, Freddy for short. Well, I couldn't say Freddie when I was a tiny tot, so it got distorted.'

'Sorry, love,' said the blonde. 'All I meant was that you could play Abanazar, the wicked uncle. You'd do that grand.'

'We couldn't put on a pantomime in the middle of summer,' said Mrs Blaine firmly. 'I shall not write that suggestion on the board.'

'Sorry I spoke,' said the blonde disagreeably. She was the wardrobe and make-up mistress and seldom got a part.

'If we're calling it the Caxton Festival,' said a solidly-built man named James Hunty, a local house-agent and a close friend of the president, 'I think, Hamilton, we ought to do something more or less in the Caxton period. What's wrong with *Saint Joan*? I could take the Earl of Warwick and. . .'

'Far too expensive a production,' said Ernest Farrow. 'Our finances would never run to it. Think of all those fifteenth-century costumes and the armour and all that.'

'Besides,' put in the youth who was responsible for the stage effects, 'think of that scene on the bank of the Loire when, by a miracle, the wind changes. Remember that pennon on the lance? If anything goes wrong with that pennon the whole point of the scene is lost and you all know what a damned draught there is on that town hall stage.'

'I do. I went all gooseflesh when I had to play Titania in the *Dream*,' said one of the girls.

'Well, you *would* play it all diaphanous,' said Melanie. 'Actually, you were hardly decent with the light behind you.'

'Some are more fortunate in their figures than others.'

'I heard some remarks passed that you wouldn't have cared for, I can tell you.'

'*Please*, ladies!' said the chairman.

'I remember that draught,' said young Tom Blaine. 'I had to play Puck stripped to the waist...'

'Which I had forbidden you to do,' said his mother, pointing her piece of blackboard chalk at him in a menacing manner.

'*Please*!' reiterated the chairman desperately. 'If you all go on like this we shall get nothing settled. Are there any further suggestions before we take the vote?'

'Bags I Saint Joan,' said Stella Walker, 'but, if you settle for that, you'll have to cut quite a lot of it. There's that boring scene in Warwick's tent between him and Cauchon, for example. Our sort of audience could never be expected to sit through that.'

'Shaw knew nothing about the Middle Ages, anyway,' said a young man named Robert Eames.

'If there are no more suggestions,' said the president desperately, 'I really think...'

'Oh, but we *must* have some more suggestions, Mr Chairman,' interpolated the scribe at the blackboard. 'To my mind we have not heard one sensible voice so far.'

'Why don't we do three one-acts,?' asked Geoffrey Channing. 'We tried that at school in my last year and they went like a bomb.'

'We tried it, too, four years ago,' said the secretary. 'It was hardly a success. The people in the first play felt that their evening was over much too soon, and those in the middle play complained that the first play hadn't got the audience sufficiently warmed up, and as for the last play...'

'Yes, I remember that last play,' said Melanie bitterly. 'I was the only woman in it and all the men had spent the first two plays in the pub and came on stage absolutely sloshed. I should think the people in the seventh row of the stalls could smell them and I had to be made love to by one of them. Ugh!'

'Why not a revue?' asked Stella Walker, giggling. 'You know – take off the politicians and some of the people in this town. It would be a riot, I'll bet.'

'It probably would cause one,' said the treasurer, 'besides letting us in for several libel actions. I definitely think we must rule out *that* suggestion.'

'I still think we ought to do a musical,' said Sybil Gartner, sticking to her guns.

'*Porgy and Bess*,' suggested Geoffrey Channing. 'I wouldn't mind blacking up in a good cause.'

'The audience would mistake us for the Black and White Minstrels,' said Robert Eames. 'They sing, too, you know.'

The chairman called the meeting to order again. Clarice Blaine wrote *Porgy and Bess* on the blackboard and added an even bigger and more offensive question mark against it than the one which already criticised *Blithe Spirit*.

'I beg your pardon if I am out of order, Mr Chairman,' said the newly-joined member, 'but what is the object of holding a Caxton Festival? He had no connection with Hampshire, had he? I thought he set up his printing-press at Westminster.'

'Ah, Dr Denbigh,' said Mrs Blaine, before the chairman could reply, 'thereby hangs a very interesting tale. We actually have a William Caxton living in our midst – well, very nearly in our midst – and as the printing-press is now five hundred years old – 1476 to 1976, you know – I decided that a festival must be held with our very own William Caxton as the principal figure. So far I have been unable to persuade him to take part, but I am determined that he can and shall be in the forefront.'

'There aren't those dreadful royalties on Gilbert and Sullivan nowadays,' said Sybil, still hopeful of getting her way by sheer persistance. 'Why don't we do *The Yeoman of the Guard*?'

There was a chorus made up in almost equal parts of approval, disapproval and suggestions for other Gilbert and Sullivan operas.

'Gilbert and Sullivan? It's been done to death on the telly.'

'All the amateur operatic societies do it.'

'You can't beat Gilbert and Sullivan if you want to fill the house.'

'*The Yeoman of the Guard* isn't funny. What about *The Mikado*?'

'*Iolanthe* for my money. That policeman song always brings the house down, so what about that?'

'You're thinking of "A policeman's lot is not a happy one".

That doesn't come in *Iolanthe*. You mean the sentry. You know – "And every little boy and gal that's born into this world alive", but now there's a Labour Party that song has lost its point, and that's true of most of Gilbert's jokes.'

'What about *The Gondoliers*? Prettier music and more amusing clothes.' So on and so forth amid pandemonium until the chairman, with more difficulty this time, once again called the meeting to order.

'We've been given plenty of ideas,' he said. 'We will take them one by one for a show of hands.'

'Excellent,' said Clarice. 'I will write up the number of votes for each one and then we can eliminate the least fancied titles and vote again upon the rest.'

'Why can't we do *The Duenna*?' demanded Sybil rebelliously.

'Your Gilbert and Sullivan suggestion is on the board, dear,' Clarice pointed out. 'Do you wish to change it? You cannot give us more than one suggestion.'

'She can't make a musical suggestion at all,' said the treasurer desperately. 'Apart from all the other expenses, the chorus, as well as the principals, would have to be costumed.'

'They can make their own dresses. The women mostly do,' retorted Sybil hotly.

'There would have to be a paid orchestra.

'Oh, nonsense! Chamber music would be quite enough in the town hall which we use. What's the matter with a violin or two, a 'cello and a piano? Surely we can rustle up those without paying them!'

'A full orchestra is absolutely essential,' persisted Ernest unhappily, 'and that means a paid conductor. It's all quite out of the question.'

'Before we commit ourselves to ruling out a musical piece,' said Dr Denbigh quietly, 'I wonder whether I might be allowed to make a suggestion? As you may or may not know, I am in charge of the music at the Chardle College of Education, so if I supply extra choristers, the full college orchestra and myself as guest conductor – all, needless to say, free of charge – is there any reason why Miss Gartner should not have her way? To my mind, a festival definitely calls for music.'

'Why, what a wonderful idea!' cried Sybil joyously. There

was a general murmur of appreciation from all those who could sing in tune and from some who could not.

'Perhaps you have a favourite piece in your mind that you would like us to perform,' said Clarice graciously, as she poised her piece of chalk.

'Certainly I have,' Denbigh coolly replied. 'I have made my own arrangement of tunes for the songs in John Gay's *The Beggar's Opera*, and it would give me enormous pleasure to see how my bits and pieces would sound in the town hall.'

'Our own composer!' breathed Clarice ecstatically. She cleaned the blackboard with a dramatic flourish. 'There is no need to take a vote, I'm sure. However – all those in favour of *The Beggar's Opera* raise your hands! Oh, splendid!'

'Bags I Polly Peachum,' said Sybil.

'Oh, but, hang it all!' protested a man. 'I do think we ought to vote on *all* the propositions. What about those of us who don't sing? Mrs Gavin, you'll support me, I'm sure.'

'But I'm sure Laura *can* sing,' said Melanie.

'She can caterwaul, you mean,' said Laura. 'Still, I do think, with all respect to Dr Denbigh and many thanks for his very sporting offer, that we ought to keep to the original agreement and vote on the various suggestions. There are at least seven soloists in *The Beggar's Opera*, so I'm all in favour of doing it, but I think we ought to vote.'

'But it will come to the same thing in the end,' said Sybil, 'so where's the sense of going through the entire list? Anyway, Clarice has cleaned the blackboard.'

'I have made my own list,' said the secretary. 'How am I directed from the chair? Shall I read the suggestions one by one?'

'Oh, Mrs Gavin is quite right, of course,' said Haynings. 'However much of a foregone conclusion it may be, we must vote as agreed. Sit down, please, Clarice, and vote with the others.'

'Very well, Hamilton,' said Mrs Blaine, seating herself uncomfortably at a very small desk. 'It is only a formality, this voting, I am sure, but it is as well to leave no loopholes for future criticism.'

'Although I am to read out the items, I take it that I may vote,' said Cyril. He cleared his throat and began to read from his list.

There were twenty members present and of these eleven voted for *The Beggar's Opera.* There were four abstentions. The rest of the voters opted for straight plays because they could see no part for themselves in a musical production.

As soon as the issue was clear, Denbigh, at the chairman's invitation, took charge of the meeting. It seemed as though he had anticipated the result of the voting, for his plans appeared to be fully developed and he explained them modestly but with an authority which brooked no argument. So sure of himself was he that his suggestions were received without demur. Even Clarice Blaine remained quiescent for once. Her only contribution was:

'I shall be stage manager, as usual, I take it, so when next we meet I hope to be told what the opera is *about*, for I have to confess I have never heard of it. You would hardly call it a classic, I suppose.'

'That, I think, is because the airs were based originally on popular tunes which would have been familiar to eighteenth-century ears, but are not what we think of as classical music,' said Denbigh courteously. 'The piece is called an opera, but there is a considerable amount of speaking interspersed with solos and duets. There is very little chorus work. In fact, a comedy with satirical undertones and including songs might be a more apt way of describing it than referring to it as an opera, Mrs Blaine.'

'It sounds very pretty and pleasant,' said Clarice graciously. '*The Beggar's Opera*! A gypsy rhapsody, perhaps?'

'No. It is set in a poor part of London.'

'Really? How very interesting. I trust there is nobody like Bill Sykes in it!'

'Oh, no. There is nobody in the least like Bill Sykes and, except for a parade of prisoners who are celebrating a stay of execution, all the personages of the drama are clean and well-dressed.'

'And I can manage the dresses without any help,' said the blonde, looking aggressively at Clarice. 'If it's period, most of 'em will have to be hired, anyway.'

CHAPTER 13

The false deduction from the twisted facts

'How did your meeting go?' Dame Beatrice enquired when Laura arrived back at the Stone House at half-past eleven that night. Laura laughed.

'We're committed to *The Beggar's Opera*,' she said. 'The voting was not unanimous because there were those among us who can't sing, so, naturally, they knew they were most unlikely to be offered parts. However, by a majority verdict the thing was carried. I'm late because Dr Denbigh, the music lecturer at Chardle College, insisted upon casting the opera then and there. Mrs Blaine is delighted. Denbigh, you see, not only promised us the assistance of the college choir and orchestra, with himself as conductor, but he's actually arranged the tunes. The idea that we have a local composer as well as a local Caxton has just about made Clarice Blaine's day. I've never seen her so bucked and so much in charity with all men.'

'Who is Mrs Blaine?'

'Who isn't she, you mean. To begin with, everybody thinks she's too autocratic, not to say infernally bossy; she's interfering, arrogant, insensitive and the most loathsome type of hypocritical do-gooder on the recording angel's blacklist. She bullies the old and the poor, runs the sycophantic Ladies' Guild (over which she rides rough-shod) and, apart from all that, is on three sub-committees of the local council. She does so-called welfare work, and I'm told she's a thorn in the flesh of the non-conformist minister whose church she attends. She's a school governor and she's a sort of one-woman *vigilante* over the factory girls' morals. I wonder they haven't lynched her before now.'

'One might almost suppose that you disliked the poor woman.'

'I do, heartily. One thing,' added Laura, grinning, 'I don't believe she's going to continue to like Denbigh as much as she does at present. I'm waiting for her to find out that he is going to boss the show without any assistance from her and I'm longing for her reactions when she reads the script of *The Beggar's Opera*. When she learns the kind of people it's about, she's going to have a heart attack if I'm any judge. By the way, they've given me the part of Mrs Peachum, so I'm only on in the first act and can come and sit with you in the audience for the rest of the time. That is if you're going to favour us with your patronage.'

'Nothing would induce me to stay away.'

'Right. I'll make sure you have a good seat for the last night, then.'

'I had some idea that you mentioned a production of *Othello*.'

'I did, but it's been shelved *pro. tem.* in favour of this Caxton Festival thing. It seems we have a William Caxton living in the neighbourhood, so what with that, and this year's being the five-hundredth anniversary of the English printing press, Clarice Blaine pressurised the Ladies' Guild into putting on a pageant and then wished this Festival business on to the dramatic society.'

'So who suggested *The Beggar's Opera*?'

'Denbigh himself. To begin with, anybody who wished could put forward a suggestion and you really ought to have been there and heard some of the ideas. Then Sybil Gartner, who's having her voice trained, put in a big word for comic opera – it was agreed, you see, that the Festival piece should be something cheerful, that's why *Othello* has been referred back. I think that man Rodney Crashaw is rather sick about it. He was to be Othello, you see, and now he won't have much of a part at all because, although he says he can sing, Denbigh offered him only a minor rôle and I think he's turned it down.'

'But *Othello* is only postponed, you say. He has his pleasure in store.'

'I don't want him to have any pleasure. He's a heel. He's got his blonde, but he makes passes at people. He's a prize nuisance.'

'I imagine that you keep him in his place.'

'I put my fist in his face once. His nose bled something shocking.'

'These Amazonian antics! "I thought the girl had been better bred!"'

'Don't pinch my lines! Oh, honestly, though, I'm delighted at the idea of being Mrs Peachum. I never expected to get a part at all, as I'm a pretty new member.'

'So Dr Denbigh has already cast the opera.'

'Oh, yes, quietly but firmly he took over the whole meeting. I should think he's a force to be reckoned with in that training college. He made all those who fancied a part to stand up and form a line so that he could get a good look at us and assess height and appearance and so forth. Then we each had to recite a nursery rhyme and sing a verse of our favourite song. After that we had to walk up and down the room in front of him.'

'And could most people manage the verse of a song?'

'They all tried except young Stella Walker. She was dying to be in it, but said she couldn't even croak. However, she is quite pretty, so Denbigh has given her two little bits and one of the others is to sing her ditties from the wings. She's bucked to death. At first Crashaw wouldn't even have a go. He's very bitter about *Othello*. There are to be three rehearsals a week for the next six weeks and Ernest Farrow, the treasurer, who's only got a tiny part right at the beginning, will play the piano for us. We shan't rehearse with the college orchestra until nearer the time.'

'Dr Denbigh seems to have had everything planned.'

'Yes. I think he was determined to do *The Beggar's Opera*. I like people who know their own minds and get things done. I offered him a lift back to the College, but he's got his own car. He calls it Lillian, after the cat in Damon Runyan's story.'

'Ah, yes, I remember. The cat became what the author describes as a rum-pot and because of this it accidentally saved a baby's life.'

'Well, Denbigh claims that his car is another rum-pot, only, instead of whisky, it drinks an alarming amount of petrol. He thinks it will be cheaper, in the long run, to scrap it and buy a newer model.'

'And you have been given a leading rôle in his production?'

'Yes, I have, and the very one I should have chosen. My word! I can just see myself! I shall be a riot. I shall have the audience rolling in the aisles, you see if I don't! Incidentally, Crashaw's blowsy blonde tried conclusions with Mrs Blaine and won.'

Dame Beatrice received her visitor with wary courtesy. She could imagine no reason why Mrs Blaine should call on her. However, she offered Clarice a chair and rang for tea.

'You won't know me from Adam – or perhaps I should say from Eve,' said the visitor.

'Oh, but, in a sense, I do,' Dame Beatrice assured her.

'Oh, well, yes, I am somewhat of a public figure, I admit.'

'Laura has spoken of you to me.'

'Laura?' Mrs Blaine looked startled.

'Laura Gavin, my friend, companion and confidential secretary.'

'Really? I assure you I had no idea. I know the names of all our members, of course, but they come from near and far and I know very few of their addresses. So dear Laura lives here.' She looked around appreciatively at the well-appointed room. 'But I thought she was *Mrs* Gavin. Is she – she is not widowed, by any chance, I hope? One likes to know that kind of thing so that one may avoid tactlessness.'

'Quite. Laura is married to an Assistant Commissioner of Police at New Scotland Yard, if it is still so called, and the marriage is a happy one.'

'Indeed? How very interesting and nice.'

'She is in London at the moment, as a matter of fact. Her husband is on annual leave.'

'Oh, really? I am sorry not to greet her, but, indeed, Dame Beatrice, it is you I came to see, and, I ought to explain, upon a begging errand. Oh, no, not for money,' Clarice hastily added, perceiving that her hostess had now assumed the expression of a benevolent snake and was making a move towards a Hepplewhite bureau-bookcase which stood against a side wall. 'Not for money at all, unless – well, as you know dear Laura so well – unless you would care to subscribe to the funds by purchasing tickets for our next performance.'

'Given by the dramatic and operatic society? I shall be delighted.'

'Thank you so much. Perhaps a tiny cheque when I go. Oh, no sugar, please.' She glanced down at her buxom figure. 'One needs to watch one's weight.' She nullified this assertion by ignoring the thin bread and butter and reaching out for one of Henri's delicious cream cakes. 'No, I really came to beg a favour of you – two favours,' she added, as though, by putting it thus, she removed any apprehension which the statement might have engendered. Dame Beatrice took a sip of tea and waited for the blow, or, rather, the two blows, to fall. 'We are preparing to honour the fifth centenary of Caxton's – of the setting up of Caxton's printing press,' Mrs Blaine went on.

'So Laura has told me.'

'What very delicious cakes these are! You do not make them yourself, by any chance?'

'No. They are of Gallic origin. My own activities, I regret to say, are purely cerebral. I should be of no practical use to the Ladies' Guild in the guise of amateur cake-maker and stall-holder.'

'Ah, yes, the Ladies' Guild,' said Clarice, taking up the cue, as Dame Beatrice had intended that she should. 'That's just it. Caxton is being obstructive, so we wondered whether – your profession, you know – your power over the mind...'

'Caxton is being obstructive? But, dear Mrs Blaine, I am a psychiatrist, not a necromancer or a medium for spirits; neither have I any personal experience of the ouija board.'

Clarice Blaine stared and then half-heartedly laughed, uncertain whether the remarks were made seriously or not.

'No, no. You don't understand,' she said. '*Our* Caxton is not the *real* Caxton, of course. He happens to bear the same name, that's all. It was his name and, of course, the date, which gave me the idea for the Ladies' Guild pageant.'

'He calls himself *William* Caxton?'

'That is his name. What makes it so interesting is that, in an amateur way, he also is a printer.'

'Yes, these bizarre occupations do seem to run in families,' said Dame Beatrice absently, her thoughts busy with A.C. Swinburne, T.E. Lawrence and now W. Caxton and R. Crashaw. She recollected herself. 'Will you take another cup of tea? And do help yourself to the cakes.'

'Thank you, yes, another cup, if you please, and, do you know, in spite of my doctor's orders, I believe I *will* have another of these delicious morsels. Well, as I was saying, it seemed such a good idea to have a Caxton pageant, but, of course, we need Caxton himself to lead it. Can you believe, though, that he refuses, absolutely *refuses* to have anything to do with it? Well, as I said to him, how can we have a Caxton pageant without Caxton?'

'You could get someone to impersonate him, could you not?'

'Oh, but, Dame Beatrice, what an anticlimax when we could get the *real man*!'

'But, dear Mrs Blaine, your Caxton is *not* the real man.'

'He must be a lineal descendant. You said yourself that these things run in families.'

'So I did. I should be interested to meet your William Caxton.'

'And compel him to do his duty and lead our pageant? How delighted I am to hear you say so! Well, that is the first of my tiresome requests got out of the way. The last time I called on him he showed me the door, but he will find that I am not to be deterred by a mere exhibition of ill-manners. I shall beard him again in the person of someone. . .' she looked with satisfaction at Dame Beatrice's sharp black eyes, claw-hands and beaky little mouth – 'someone whom he will find impossible to withstand.'

'Well, I promise nothing. However, in so good a cause as the Caxton pageant,' said Dame Beatrice, with a crocodile grin, 'I shall do my best to persuade this young man. Is he young?'

'In his thirties, I would say.'

'To a centenarian like myself that must seem young.'

Mrs Blaine's large and arrogant face wore an expression to which it was unaccustomed, an expression of doubt and perplexity. She essayed what she hoped was a light laugh and decided to change the subject.

'We come now,' she said, as she had said so often when taking the chair at her Ladies' Guild, 'to an equally important but totally different matter.' Her face changed its expression to one with which Hamilton Haynings would have been uneasily familiar. 'It concerns my second request and is a matter of extreme urgency and considerable delicacy. Dame Beatrice, the Caxton Festival cannot produce *The Beggar's Opera*.'

'I thought Dr Denbigh was producing it,' said Dame Beatrice innocently.

'You do not grasp my meaning. Neither I nor the Ladies' Guild can countenance the production of such a piece in Chardle. It is not only vulgar, it is immoral.'

'Dear me! What *could* poor John Gay have been thinking of to write such a thing?'

'I can tell you what he was thinking of. He was thinking of the criminal classes. He was thinking of thieves and highwaymen; of the receivers of stolen goods; of pickpockets and prostitutes; of illegitimate children and of co-habitation outside the sanctity of marriage. The piece has not one single uplifting or ennobling theme or thought. It is disgracefully improper. My son, a child of sixteen years, has been given the part of Filch, a pickpocket, and words cannot express the horror I felt when, upon glancing through the copy of the words with which, at my request, Dr Denbigh had supplied me, my eye lighted upon one of the speeches which my son will be required to make. I am fully and disapprovingly aware, Dame Beatrice, that we live in a decadent and so-called permissive age, but surely. . .'

'I am convinced that you need have no fear,' said Dame Beatrice, as words appeared, for once in her masterful career, to fail Mrs Blaine. 'I am familiar with the text of *The Beggar's Opera* and I have no doubt that Dr Denbigh will sufficiently expurgate the text to make it acceptable to the Ladies' Guild and the other unsullied minds of Chardle. Sir Nigel Playfair himself thought it better not to include those lines in your son's speech to which I think you refer.'

'I am relieved to hear it, but that does not alter the fact that this profligate piece extols and approves the drunken skylarkings of. . .'

'Pimps, trulls and trollops?'

'You appear to take the matter light-heartedly, Dame Beatrice!'

'Surely that is the way John Gay intended it to be taken?'

'But the characters he depicts! I repeat – highwaymen, pickpockets, receivers of stolen goods! Every man in it, including the prison authorities, is an infamous scoundrel. As for the so-called "ladies of the town", in other words the drabs of Drury Lane. . .'

'Lewkner's Lane,' amended Dame Beatrice solemnly. 'In fact, we are told that some of the ladies came from as far away as Hockley-in-the-Hole. Macheath must have had great charm and, "although the bank hath stopped payment", to have been generously free with his money.'

'You appear to be *extremely* familiar with the text, Dame Beatrice,' said poor Clarice, striving vainly, although valiantly, to keep disapproval out of her voice, 'but perhaps you have used it as an exercise in the psychology of human depravity. The frailty of human nature. . .'

'Particularly the frailty of women, to whom the author gives, in the person of Mrs Peachum (to be played, to her great delight, by Laura) some excellent advice. May I quote?'

'Please do,' said Mrs Blaine stiffly, 'if you see any point in doing so.'

'She says,' continued Dame Beatrice in her beautiful voice, ' "Yes, indeed, the sex is frail. But the first time a woman is frail she should be somewhat nice, methinks, for then or never is the time to make her fortune." So pleasant to have the word "nice" correctly used, don't you think? The speech of the eighteenth century was so eminently superior to our present-day slipshod methods of using and misusing the language.'

'I am not aware of being slipshod or of misusing the language,' said Clarice, 'and I still think the piece is utterly unsuitable for public performance in Chardle.'

'You are of Jeeves's opinion, perhaps, that "what pleases the London public is not always so acceptable to the rural mind. The metropolitan touch sometimes proves a trifle too exotic for the provinces". May I ask whether you are alone in your disapproval of the piece?'

'Unfortunately, this appears to be so.'

'Then I suppose there is nothing to be done but to accept the democratic principle that the wishes of the majority must be respected.'

'Democracy is the most inefficient form of government ever invented!' snorted Clarice angrily.

'That is so true; and yet, if *vox populi* is *vox dei*, who are we to set ourselves against it?' asked her hostess.

The visitor rose to take her leave. She tore a leaf out of a tiny notebook and handed it to Dame Beatrice.

'It is good of you to promise to visit Caxton. Here is his address,' she said abruptly. 'It is a little off the beaten track. The best way is to take the Brockenhurst road and enquire at Buckett's farm. Caxton is their tenant. I have to thank you for a most delicious tea.'

'She may have enjoyed a delicious tea, but I do not think she saw mine as a delicious mind,' said Dame Beatrice to Laura when the latter returned. 'As for giving my kind co-operation in the matter of attempting to persuade William Caxton to lead the Ladies' Guild through the streets of Chardle, I would not have agreed except that I want an excuse to meet this aptly-named printer.'

'Do I gather you didn't much take to our Clarice?'

'I am sure she is the worthiest of women and, no doubt, a good wife and mother.'

'But, as a companion on a walking tour she wouldn't be exactly your first choice. Oh, well, we don't always recognise or appreciate the highest when we see it. She's a bit cheesed off, you know, because Denbigh has ridden rough-shod over her. She's accustomed to try to produce our shows as well as stage-manage them, I'm told, so I do rather hope you didn't tease her, but I'm rather afraid you might have done. Did she touch you for a subscription?'

'In the beginning, yes, but at parting she refused it. I think the refusal was a mark of her displeasure. In fact, I am quite sure it was.'

'Too right, I'd say. Well, you've agreed to tackle Caxton, it seems, so do you want me to accompany you on your visit to this wild man of the woods?'

'If you will agree to leave all the talking to me, I shall be glad of your company. I have the liveliest suspicions concerning him.'

'What is he? – clad in goat skins, like Robinson Crusoe, or a demander of cheese, like poor Ben Gunn?'

'Neither, I trust. Does the name William Caxton convey anything to you, apart from the printing press and the date 1476?'

'Convey anything to me? No. Why should it? There are probably dozens of Caxtons in the telephone book and William isn't exactly an uncommon Christian name.'

'You relieve my mind.'

Laura stared hard at her employer. 'What *is* all this?' she asked.

Dame Beatrice cackled. 'Just a foolish notion I entertained; an idea which you have now, I am glad to say, relegated to its proper sphere, which is *limbo*.'

Laura looked dissatisfied.

'You don't often get ideas which have to be treated like unbaptised infants,' she remarked. '*Limbo* is where *they're* supposed to go. You wouldn't care to come clean and give me the gist of your thoughts, I suppose?'

'I am ashamed of them. The clear light of your commonsense has shown me how foolish they are.'

Laura went into the library, the adjoining room, to write to the handsome husband whom she had recently left in London, but, instead of beginning her letter, she scribbled on the blotting-pad – an anachronism in an age of ball-point pens – *William Caxton, William Wallace, William Shakespeare, William Wilberforce, William of Orange, William Wordsworth, William Butler Yeats, William Congreve, William of Wykeham*. She tapped on the blotter as she studied the list. Then she read it aloud. When she came to the last name she repeated it and then uttered it a third time. She scribbled all across the list of names, took a piece of writing paper from a drawer and began her letter to Assistant Commissioner Rober Gavin.

When she had stamped the envelope and put it in the tray ready for posting, she went back to Dame Beatrice, who was industriously but purposelessly knitting.

'William of Wykeham. William Wayneflete. Wayneflete College. Alfriston C. Swinburne, Thaddeus E. Lawrence, William Caxton,' said Laura. 'Am I right? But it's a bit far-fetched, don't you think?'

'I am sure of it, and I have already confessed as much.' Dame Beatrice cast aside the repulsive network of pale mauve wool which she had been knitting and added, 'Let us think no more about it. When shall we go and see this young man?'

'The tooter the sweeter.'

They set off next day, Laura driving, took the Brockenhurst road and branched off past Buckett's farm, but did not call there. The open common gave place to woods and a little stream. The car crossed a narrow bridge. Beyond this there was open forest and then a boundary lane bordered by a couple of shallow ponds. Some ponies were grazing and beyond them was the cottage which Laura, whose knowledge of the Forest was encyclopaedic, had found easily enough from the address which Mrs Blaine had left with Dame Beatrice.

From the narrow road which the car had been following after it had crossed the bridge, not much more than the roof and chimneys of the cottage could be seen, for it was down in a dip. From the road an ill-defined path made by the feet of pedestrians across the turf could be seen leading to a wicket-gate. Laura pulled up off the narrow road and she and her employer took the path to the cottage.

It was in a small enclosure which could hardly be called a garden and in this space there was an open shed containing a motor-cycle and an old mangle. The cottage itself was in need of a coat of paint. The door to it was open and through the doorway came the sound of song.

Laura called out unnecessarily, 'Anybody home?' and a young man came to the open doorway.

'Somebody asking for me?' he enquired. Dame Beatrice came forward.

'Mr William Caxton, I believe,' she said. The young man smiled at her.

'If you've come on behalf of the ladies of the town,' he said, 'you've wasted your time, I'm afraid. I have no intention whatever of appearing in their Caxton pageant.'

'Not even if I am willing to give you the printing of all posters, tickets and programmes for the Festival play?'

His face changed. He looked alert and interested.

'That's different,' he said. 'Would you do that?'

'On condition of your appearing in the pageant, of course. Payment will be made when the pageant is over and you have taken part.'

'Trusting, aren't you?' He grinned disarmingly. 'O.K. I accept. I can do with the money. Incidentally, my work is good and not cheap. Come inside and I'll give you an estimate.

'Forgive me for mentioning it,' said Laura, when they were back in the car, 'but surely Clarice Blaine didn't authorise you to *bribe* the chap, did she?'

'No, and I have not committed her or the Ladies' Guild or the dramatic society to any financial transactions. I intend to pay for the printing myself if this obliging William Caxton undertakes to appear in the pageant. I feel that I owe Mrs Blaine something for having shocked her so deeply by my refusal to lend my support to her ban on *The Beggar's Opera*. Besides, I have satisfied myself of one thing.'

'I'll take a guess. You know now that Caxton is really Caxton, although I bet it's simply a trade name to advertise the fact that he has this printing press. And you also know that he isn't Thaddeus E. Lawrence, not to mention Alfriston C. Swinburne.'

'You are right, but you had already convinced me that my suspicions were foolish and irrational. Still, it is always as well to be sure.'

'But our professional blonde, who opted for a pantomime as our Festival offering, *could* be Coralie St Malo,' said Laura. 'No, of course she couldn't, any more than Caxton could be Lawrence.'

> 'Sure, these are but imaginary wiles,
> And Lapland sorcerers inhabit here',

quoted Dame Beatrice, with an eldritch cackle. 'There still remains R. Crashaw, of course.'

Laura looked suspiciously at her employer, convinced that she was being teased, but unable to see the point of the teasing.

CHAPTER 14

There are enough pickers and stealers in this town.

Among few sets of people do envy and jealousy flourish more lushly and with more rapid growth than among the members of an amateur dramatic and operatic society. This generalisation does not apply to those who are given the leading rôles, of course. So far as the Chardle group was concerned, the three leading women players were well satisfied with the parts which Denbigh had allotted them. Laura was delighted to have been given Mrs Peachum, Sybil Gartner had expected to play Polly and had not been disappointed and, although she had her detractors, Melanie Cardew, that raddled tragedy queen, was pleased at first and (although nothing would have induced her to say so) surprised at having been asked to play Lucy Lockit, a part which, except for her defection, would have been offered to Marigold Tench, who had a better voice.

That Polly Peachum had been given to Sybil nobody queried. It was known (for she frequently referred to the fact) that she took singing lessons and (like Cora Bellinger, whose voice could bring down plaster from the ceiling) was 'studying for opera'. Besides this, she knew that she had a good stage presence. She was, in fact, a personable enough young woman although she had hard eyes and an obstinate chin. However, she also had an attractive figure, including what Damon Runyan would describe as 'bumps here and there where a doll is entitled to have bumps', and there was no doubt that, as Laura put it, she could out-voice the rest of the company even when she was singing *pianissimo*, for hers was a high, clear soprano, piercing rather than sweet, and of undoubted power.

Over Laura's own part in the production there had also been no envious murmurings. For one thing, there was no other obvious choice for Mrs Peachum and, for another, the character, dominant in the first Act, does not appear at all during the rest of the performance, a fact to deter the exhibitionists, the self-assertive and the merely vain. What was more, in Denbigh's production it was decreed that whoever played Mrs Peachum should take over the dull and thankless office of prompter for the last two Acts. The Lucy Lockit, who did not come on stage until Act Two, was to occupy the prompter's stool for Act One before handing over to Mrs Peachum at the first interval while the stage was being re-set for the scene at the Newgate tavern, but that ended her responsibility.

Unlike Sir Nigel Playfair's classic revival of *The Beggar's Opera* in the 1920s, which was produced against only one background, the Chardle production was to enjoy various changes of scene, for with amateurs, as Denbigh knew, every dog must have his day and this applied as much to the stage carpenters and the scene-painters as to the actors themselves, so that the scene was to be changed not only between the Acts, but even between the two scenes in Act Two and the three scenes in Act Three. This took time, a fact which became of considerable importance later.

Apart from those allotted to Laura, Sybil and Melanie, there were only minor rôles for the women and, once the three principal male rôles were settled, the men were in like case. There was no obvious candidate, moreover, for the principal male part, that of the highwayman Macheath, so, after some misgivings, Denbigh had chosen young Cyril Wincott, but more for his tall figure and handsome countenance than because of his dramatic and musical gifts. The choice was put down by his detractors to favouritism on the score that Cyril was a schoolmaster and therefore in Denbigh's camp, but this was untrue.

Cyril's position, therefore, was a less happy one than Sybil's or Laura's, for whereas they had no detractors, Cyril had more than one. The president of the society, Hamilton Haynings, the possessor of a foghorn bass-baritone whose resonance, his critics agreed among themselves, would have been better employed on a tug on the Thames rather than in the confined space of the

Chardle town hall, had expected to be able to pull his rank and obtain the leading man's part. He had been fobbed off (in his own opinion) with Lockit, Lucy's jailor father, and his lines had been cut to restrict him to very short appearances with his daughter, with Macheath and with Peachum, Polly's father. He was given no solo at all and his only contribution to the musical side of the affair was a bawling duet in which, Denbigh privately considered, his voice could do little harm.

Peachum, a meaty part which, in lieu of playing Macheath, Hamilton would have accepted with good grace, had been given to James Hunty, the possessor of a baritone voice of good although untrained quality which he himself considered would have suited the part of Macheath far better than did Cyril's light and pleasant tenor.

'Macheath was never meant for a tenor,' he said plaintively to Marigold Tench who, bitterly regretful of her walk-out from a meeting earlier on, persisted in haunting the rehearsals in a sick mood of masochistic self-punishment.

'You couldn't play Macheath, not with *your* waistline,' said Marigold, displaying the reverse of the medal and turning sadistic. There were also others, as Laura soon found out, who were restless and dissatisfied. She had been mistaken, for one thing, in assuming, on too little evidence, that young Stella Walker was pleased with the two tiny parts of Jenny Diver and Diana Trapes. She was soon in the same camp as the blonde woman who had opted for a pantomime. The blonde, like Marigold, also insisted upon turning up at rehearsals, ostensibly to work out the costumes which would be required. She also decided to assist Farrow by turning over the pages of the score for him. It was in manuscript and not easy for the pianist to follow. Moreover, it was on separate sheets of paper which were madly inclined to flutter to the floor when anybody handled them with insufficient care. After the first two rehearsals, in fact, Ernest, living up to his name, learnt the tunes by heart and thus rendered the blonde's officious assistance unnecessary. Apart from this, Haynings tackled her with so much belligerence that she thought it well to apologise and to behave herself at all subsequent rehearsals, which she still insisted upon attending.

It had been arranged that, until the cast was word-perfect and had learnt the songs, Denbigh would not take over the rehearsals. The 'words' rehearsals for the society's productions had usually taken place in Clarice Blaine's house with coffee and biscuits to follow, but she had issued no invitation to the cast of *The Beggar's Opera* to invade her drawing-room. This attitude was to mark her resentment at being turned down as stage manager and her dire disapproval of the piece, but her excuse (for even this autocratic lady felt bound to explain so blatant a departure from custom) was that she had no piano, an excuse which, at a words-only rehearsal, hardly made sense.

All the rehearsals, until Denbigh took them over, were held, therefore, in the small, draughty hall of a local primary school, the hiring of which was cheap because its amenities were so few. Ernest, who had not dared to complain about Mabelle van Pieter's behaviour at the piano, did complain bitterly (and with reason) about the instrument itself. It was out of tune, two of the notes made no sound at all and it was on castors so that, if anybody leaned against it, and this usually meant a soloist who had come over to expostulate with the pianist, it made a disconcerting right-angled turn and left the embarrassed and fuming Ernest playing on air instead of on the keyboard.

'It's good for the poor chap to have something inanimate to curse about,' Laura informed Dame Beatrice, 'because he's too much of a rabbit to tackle anything human, either male or female. Anyway, come to that, most of us are at the stage of thinking before we speak and then not saying it. I even listen patiently to our blonde bomb-shell, the slightly overpowering (where she buys her perfume I can't think, unless it's privately imported from Port Said or somewhere), the very ripe Mabelle van Pieter.'

'You listen patiently to her? Why, what has she to say which requires patience in the listener?'

'Well, she claims to be a pro., you see, and I think it's true. She tells me I "should ought to broaden out the part, dear". Personally I think I've broadened it as far as it will stretch. She has forearms like a navvy, a spirited vocabulary and, apart from a lively hatred of Haynings since he, by no means mincing his own words, fought her to a standstill in a verbal battle last week, she gets on reasonably well with everybody, apart from giving them her unasked-for professional advice and leaping out from the wings in the middle of a scene to measure busts and hips.'

'All very well-intentioned, no doubt.'

'*She* may be well-intentioned, but there are those among us who are not. Even young Stella Walker, who seemed so pleased with her two little bits of parts, has begun to step high, wide and plentiful.'

This was true, for Stella had become a very disgruntled young lady.

'If only we'd settled on a straight play,' she said at the beginning of the fifth rehearsal, 'which, after all, was what nearly all of us wanted, I might have been given a decent part. I mean, I may not be able to sing, but I can act Sybil Gartner's head off. Do you know how many speeches I've got as Jenny Diver? Three! And only one solo – and even *that* I only mime, while Melanie Cardew sings it from the wings. And it ought to be *six* speeches and *two* songs! I do think it's wrong of him to mess up the script like this. And even the three speeches he *has* left me have all been shortened.'

'My part has been cut, too,' said Melanie, who overheard her. 'The parts of Polly and Lucy ought to be of equal importance, but they're *not*. And who wants to sing other people's songs off-stage? Besides, the thing doesn't suit my voice and who on earth can sing a line like "The gamesters and lawyers are jugglers alike," I should wish to know?' She walked over to the piano and began to berate poor Ernest whom the blonde had long since abandoned. Her place had been taken by Marigold Tench.

'Then there's the Diana Trapes part,' went on Stella to anybody who was listening. 'That's been cut, too. He's taken out *all* her main speeches and just left me with four little bits to say, and two of those have been cut to a single line. And again there's only one solo instead of two. If it wasn't for letting the rest of the cast down, I'd opt out and make him find somebody else to take my place. Anyway, if Melanie is to sing my songs, why can't *I* be Lucy? I'm sure I'd *look* the part better than she does. She's *much* too old for it.'

Stella might not have been able to sing, but she had a vibrant, carrying speaking-voice and Melanie, who had strolled away after criticising Ernest's rendering of her accompaniments, came over to her.

'Thank you very much,' she said venomously. 'If, after that, you conceited little beast, you think I'm going to sing your solos from the wings while you mime the words like a monkey catching fleas, you may as well think again. Get somebody else to do it.'

'I think I'd better, if that's how you feel about it,' said Stella, coming up and tossing her abundant red-gold hair almost in Melanie's face. 'In any case, nobody is going to believe that your strident trumpetings are coming from my larynx.'

'No. You say your words like a child with tonsillitis.'

'Perhaps Laura Gavin would sing for me,' said Stella, not relishing this description of her vocal chords. 'She'll be off-stage in the second and third Acts, anyway, because she's going to prompt when Act One is over, and I hope you fluff and have to be prompted good and loud.'

'She's a contralto, and Jenny Diver and Diana Trapes are written for mezzos in Denbigh's version,' said Marigold who, from sheer pique at having walked herself out of a part, had familiarised herself with the words and music of the opera. '*I'll* stand in the wings and sing for you if you like.'

However, the opera got under way in some sort of fashion and Laura, who, without ostentation or what she described as 'throwing her weight about' had been accepted as leader and arbiter during this trying time, was able to telephone the College and inform Philip Denbigh that she thought the company was ready for him to take over the rehearsals and that Hamilton Haynings agreed with her on the matter.

There was one member of the society who, not expecting to be given a part at all, had joyously snapped up the very minor rôle of Filch the pickpocket, although, to his mother's relief, his best lines (as he thought them) had not only been cut, but had been removed altogether from the script, and this was the young lad Tom Blaine. In spite, however, of Denbigh's concession to local good taste with regard to her son's dialogue, Tom's mother continued to do her best to sabotage the success of the production.

For all the previous shows which the society had put on she had bludgeoned her Ladies' Guild not only into buying tickets for themselves, their families and their friends, but in helping to fabricate the costumes for the various plays and in providing tea and cakes for sale during the intervals.

On this occasion, however, she declined to ask the Ladies' Guild to provide any of this valuable help. She could not, in conscience, she said, persuade people to assist at a project of which she so violently disapproved. Apart from that, the Guild had its hands completely full. The pageant also needed dressing. She added that her Young People's Helpful Band would not be doing their usual rounds of house-to-house touting for the sale of tickets, either, another useful service she had organised in previous years.

'I would not soil their young minds,' she said, 'by letting them know that such a piece was under contemplation.'

'Oh, well, if the Ladies' Guild won't help out, I suppose it means more hiring of costumes than we usually need to do,' said poor Ernest Farrow. 'Still, I suppose, for this production, if it's going to look like anything at all, we'd have to hire most of the stuff anyway. That's the worst of a period piece. I'll have to ask the principals to pay for the hire of their own outfits, as usual, but I'm worried about the sale of tickets. The Ladies' Guild are usually good for fifty or sixty of the best seats, although they *do* expect them for the Saturday night performance when we could probably sell them anyway. Then, of course, those Young People have been no end useful in getting rid of those tickets which always hang fire, especially for the second night. We shall sadly miss them.'

'Oh, well, it can't be helped,' said Hamilton Haynings, 'not but what I felt, from the beginning, that it was a mistake to leave choice of piece and all the casting to Denbigh. We must all do our best to make the thing a success, that's all.'

'Success depends on the size of the audience,' said Ernest. 'Everybody plays better when the hall is full. Nothing is more daunting than playing to rows of empty seats, so do pressurise people into buying tickets, all of you. Don't stand any nonsense from people who say they'll "think about it". Oh, and do have plenty of change about you, then there is no excuse for people who tell you they have "nothing smaller than a five-pound note". I'm giving everybody twenty top-price tickets to get rid of, and *please*,' he added pathetically, 'if you can't get anybody else to buy them, I do *beg* of you to sub up for them yourselves and *give* them away. We've got to have the money and we've got to have an audience. I'm sure you all appreciate that.'

'It's all very well for the principals,' said Stella, 'but what about the rest of us? I can't afford to buy twenty seats, and nobody I know is going to pay fifty p. to see me in a more or less walking-on part.'

'Well, do what you can,' urged Ernest. 'Time for all good men to come to the aid of the party, eh?'

'And what about the College yobbos? Will they each sell twenty tickets?' demanded Geoffrey Channing, who had been given the part, as had his friend Robert Eames, of a member of Macheath's gang of footpads. As the rest of the gang was to consist entirely of Denbigh's students, there was a point to his question and he was supported shrilly by Stella, since most of the ladies of the town were also from the college choir.

'You bet they won't,' she said.

'Oh, Denbigh will see to all that. No doubt their parents will come,' said Ernest, making an optimistic statement which he himself did not believe.

'Well, I think it's all very unfair,' said Stella mutinously, 'and, anyway, I think a committee should have decided who ought to have the parts. That's what we've always done and it's much the best way.'

'It also wastes a great deal of time,' said Sybil. 'It was far better to leave it to just one person, especially as he's being so useful to us.'

'Helpful to you, perhaps,' said Marigold Tench. 'Personally, I think there should have been proper auditions. As it was, the whole cast was settled in a matter of minutes, without any proper preliminaries at all. Of course, if you're all content to let the latest-joined member ride rough-shod over you, I've nothing more to say.'

'Thank goodness for that,' said Melanie, turning her tragic eyes upwards.

'In any case, Marigold,' said Cyril, 'you've nothing to beef about if you haven't been given a part. You chose to walk yourself off and wash your hands of the production, didn't you?'

'Oh, if she wants a part she can have mine,' said Melanie. 'I'm sure I'm sick to death of these sob-stuff rôles. I wish I could swop with Laura. I'd love to do a bit of low comedy for a change.'

'Just as you like,' said Laura, 'if the producer doesn't object.'

'*I* object!' said James Hunty. 'Either I play Act One opposite Laura, or I don't play it at all.'

'There's been enough kissing goes by favour in this production already,' said the bearded Rodney Crashaw. He looked accusingly and spitefully at Cyril Wincott, who grinned infuriatingly at him and whistled Denbigh's setting of *Over the hills and far away.*

'In any case,' said Hamilton Haynings, 'we can't start chopping and changing now, and there's no sense in picking out the parts we'd *like* to play. I confess I'm not exactly in love with the part of Lockit, but we have to be reasonable and back up Denbigh's mistakes (if he's made any) as best we can. We gave him *carte blanche* and we can't go back on it.'

'By the way,' said Laura to James Hunty, 'what's all this about Melanie wanting to play a comic part? I was under the impression that she saw herself as the Duse of this day and age.'

'She's become that creep Crashaw's leading lady. Didn't you know? I think she's a prize fool, but it isn't my business to tell her so.'

'Our platinum blonde isn't going to be pleased.'

'Too true. A *ménage à trois* is hardly likely to be *her* cup of tea!'

'Is it serious? – Crashaw and Melanie, I mean.'

'She's crazy about him. She told my wife so.'

'Oh, well, she'll live and learn, I suppose.'

'She must be full of the joys of spring if she wants to play comedy. Anyway, don't you dare give way to her, Mistress Peachum.'

CHAPTER 15

Simple ignorance can be cured by simple truth
Spoken with sincerity.

Between them, Laura with goodhumour and commonsense, Hamilton Haynings by the exercise of his authority, gradually got the better of the saboteurs, so the last half-dozen rehearsals, leading up to what might be called the sub-dress rehearsal, saw *The Beggar's Opera* beginning to take shape.

By the time Denbigh was informed that the company had cut its teeth and was ready for him, the warring factions had not only given up the struggle for power but were as anxious as anybody else that the production should be a success. As history has shown, there is nothing so powerful as a common enemy to bring private vendettas to an end, and this unifying force was provided by Clarice Blaine.

She had spoken at public meetings, she had written letters to the local press, she had asked questions at the sessions of the Chardle District Council, she had repeated those questions at meetings of the local rate-payers' association and she had lobbied the local church dignitories.

The results were that the literary, dramatic and operatic society closed ranks and that the general public bought tickets for all three performances of the opera in the lively anticipation that they were going to attend something in the nature of a cross between the Folies Bergères, a strip-show of unusual daring, a Babylonian orgy and the less presentable aspects of a witches' sabbath.

'The tickets have never gone so well as early as this,' said an exultant Ernest Farrow, as members clustered round him to ask for more to sell.

'Clarice Blaine ought to go in for advertising,' said Laura to Dame Beatrice. 'However, I've managed to snaffle a couple of dockets in the front row for the third night. If nobody needs prompting during the Thursday and Friday performances, I've told Denbigh I shall sit in front with you on the Saturday when my part is over.'

'William Caxton came here while you were at this evening's rehearsal,' said Dame Beatrice, 'and asked where he should take the posters he has printed.'

'I suppose Denbigh had better have them. If Caxton has made as good a job of them as he did of the tickets, Denbigh will be glad to have them stuck up outside the town hall.'

'Mrs Blaine has written briefly but politely to thank me for the pageant posters. I gather that we are unlikely, however, to have her company at the town hall.'

'We certainly shan't. She's been gunning for weeks to get the opera boycotted if not actually outlawed. The result is that we look like being booked solid for all three performances. In fact, I believe we could run for a week if we liked. Sweet are the uses of the English resolve to see smut where none is intended or, for the matter of that, provided. Our *Beggar's Opera* is as chaste as ice, but, fortunately, the prospective audience doesn't know that.'

'And the music?'

'Denbigh has borrowed freely from Frederic Austin, he says, and the result is a lively, tuneful romp. I don't think whatever the audience expects, that anybody will be disappointed with the songs.'

The disappointment, when it came, was to Cyril Wincott. The school of which this handsome Macheath was such an ornament had acquired a trampoline and two or three of the younger members of staff were agog to try it out. Unfortunately, after school closed on the evening of the third rehearsal at the College, at which the full college orchestra and chorus, as well as the principals, were to be present, Cyril, taking a bet that he would soar higher in the air than the others, won his bet, but landed on the edge of the trampoline, fell awkwardly and broke his right leg.

Denbigh, at the College rehearsal, received the news with

resignation. He was not unduly distressed. At this stage of the rehearsals everybody knew all the dialogue and all the songs, and he thought that to replace Cyril with one of the others would be far from impossible.

There was no lack of claimants for the part. Denbigh, anxious to show no bias, asked these to sing a duet with Sybil, the Polly Peachum. Privately he was determined not to move James Hunty, who was shaping up well in the part of Polly's father, and he was equally determined not to allow Hamilton Haynings's foghorn voice (well enough in the part of the jailor Lockit) to ruin Macheath's solos or the duets with Sybil.

Having given these two and the youthful Geoffrey Channing and Robert Eames their chance and having even tried out the diffident Ernest Farrow in the part, he shook his head regretfully and said, 'I don't quite think so, you know. I really think I had better let my top music student, who has had some experience, conduct the orchestra and I'll take the part myself.'

At this the silence which had fallen on the disappointed contestants was broken by Rodney Crashaw. He had heard of Cyril's accident and had decided to present himself at the rehearsal openly instead of in the clandestine manner he had previously employed. He came up to the front of the platform and said, with carefully simulated diffidence:

'I think the players, if not the orchestra, would be less than happy were you not to wield the conductor's bâton, Dr Denbigh. I wonder whether, before you come to a final decision, you would allow me to try a duet with Miss Gartner.'

'So long as the duet is confined to the stage and no private rehearsals are permitted,' muttered Sybil to Laura, as they waited in the wings.

'Would you mind trying over *Were I laid on Greenland's coast*, Miss Gartner?' asked Denbigh.

'Righto,' Sybil replied. 'Anything to oblige.' But at the conclusion of the duet she said, 'I'd be quite happy with that.'

'So would I,' said Denbigh. 'Right. Let's have the Beggar and the Player on stage and try a complete run-through.'

The college orchestra was already tuning up and the college 'extras' in the persons of Macheath's gang, the ladies of the town and the other minor rôles which the students were to fill, were ready and waiting when there were 'noises off' and, to everybody's astonishment, Mrs Blaine turned up with Caxton in tow and seated herself, with him beside her, near the back of the room.

'I want to be sure that the dialogue is *audible*,' she said. 'Some of my friends told me, after our last production, that they had difficulty in *hearing* some of the characters. I shall call out *at once* if I fail to catch what anybody utters.'

'Pardon me, Mrs Blaine,' said Denbigh crisply, 'but I can allow no interference with my rehearsal. You are welcome to sit and listen, of course, but the only interruptions will come from me, if you please. I am sure you understand. Beginners ready?'

The Beggar and the Player took the stage, the Player called upon the orchestra to 'play away the overture' and the rehearsal, with James Hunty, Laura, young Tom Blaine (whose voice had broken to a light, immature, but rather attractive tenor), Sybil as Polly and the saturnine bearded Crashaw as Macheath, got off to a flourishing start.

Philip Denbigh allowed the whole act to run its course, praised the players, took them all through it again, including the overture, and this time called for frequent stops while he made his comments and asked for repetition of lines, parts of solos and stage business. The clock crept from seven to eight and from eight to nine before he called for Act Two.

This went better than Laura, who was prompting, had expected. She had very little to do. This time Denbigh, who must have rehearsed his choral students very carefully, did not ask Macheath's gang or the ladies of the town to repeat any part of their performance, but began his criticism and advice only after the entrance of Peachum with the constables who had come to arrest Macheath.

At eleven o'clock he declared the rehearsal over and added that next time they would begin with Act Three. He hoped he had not kept them too late and congratulated them upon their efforts. Mrs Blaine had long ago taken young Tom home in his father's car, but Caxton had stayed on and at the end of the rehearsal he approached Laura and begged for a lift back to his cottage.

'Thought you'd brought your motor-bike,' she said, not at all anxious to be taken so far out of her way so late at night.

'I've run out of petrol,' he said.

'Well, there's an all-night garage in the town not a quarter of a mile from here,' said Hamilton Haynings, joining them.

'Oh, all right, then. Thanks,' said Caxton, walking away.

'Thank *you*,' said Laura to Haynings. 'The last thing I wanted was to drive into the depths of the Forest at this time of night.'

'He had a damned cheek to ask a woman to go,' said James Hunty. 'Why couldn't he have asked one of the chaps? What was he doing here, anyway? He doesn't belong to our lot.'

'Mrs Blaine brought him. She wants him to speak a little piece at our show to boost her pageant.'

'She *would*!' He accompanied Laura to her car. 'Damned cheek!' he said again; but whether he was referring to Clarice Blaine or to Caxton, she did not know and did not ask him.

'Very decent of Haynings to chip in,' she said to Dame Beatrice when she got back to the Stone House. 'Saved me quite an embarrassing moment, although I'm not sure I want him as a father-figure. Anyway, I certainly wasn't prepared to take Caxton home, but one doesn't really like refusing. Had he been one of the cast it might have been different, but actually he had no right to be at the rehearsal at all, and I'm surprised Philip Denbigh let him stay.'

'You say he came with Mrs Blaine?'

'Even so, she had no right to bring him. I suppose she's so pleased to have got him for her pageant that she's determined to keep her hooks on him. And she *wouldn't* have got him but for your noble action in paying for all that printing. I must say he's made a good job of it.'

'Yes, indeed, and at a far from extortionate price.'

The next rehearsal began, as Denbigh had promised, with Act Three. Laura handled the prompt-script and was surprised by the high standard of performance reached by Sybil and Melanie as Macheath's rival wives. They had always been adequate in these rôles, but, playing opposite Crashaw, they had improved their performance a hundred per cent and had electrified the rest of the cast.

'Well, now,' said Denbigh, when Macheath had been reprieved and the last chorus had been sung, 'I think, under the circumstances, we had better have a complete run-through just to make sure Mr Crashaw is not going to muddle the rest of you in the first two acts. We'll leave out the solos and just take the spoken words and the stage "business", and then I think we ought to have one more complete rehearsal, this time at the town hall, before the dress rehearsal. Is there anybody who can't manage Saturday afternoon? The dress rehearsal proper is on Monday, and I shall need you all to be punctual. Six-thirty sharp, please, for a curtain-up at seven-thirty, and you had better arrange to be prepared to stay until midnight. Dress rehearsals always take about twice as long as anybody thinks they are going to, and I believe a photographer is expected, so that means more delay. And do, please, look after yourselves. It will be a disaster if anybody else falls down and breaks an arm or a leg.'

'So there it is,' said Laura, on the Saturday morning. 'I'm very sorry indeed for young Wincott. He was very keen on his part and it's rotten luck on him having to spend weeks in hospital. On the other hand, we're getting a much better singer and actor in this heel Crashaw. His voice is quite decent. He's had a show down with Denbigh, though.'

'Oh, really? I thought you had just reported that he was good in the part.'

'It isn't that. It's his beard. Denbigh wanted him to shave it off, but he won't.'

'A beard would be quite in keeping with the part, would it not?'

'Denbigh doesn't like beards. However, Crashaw claims that he grew his to cover up a very unsightly scar. I don't believe it; I think he's just simply attached to the beastly thing.'

'And is to remain attached to it?'

'Yes. Denbigh gave in. Under the circumstances he could hardly do anything else, I suppose. By the way, expect me home in the small hours of tomorrow morning. We're going to do a preliminary dress rehearsal at the town hall this evening so that the wardrobe mistress can vet us.'

'Who is this talented woman?'

'Oh, didn't I tell you? She is Mabelle van Pieter, our cataclysmic blonde. She's also one of the ladies of the town and, if you ask me, I'd say that against Stella Walker and the damsels from the College of Education, she'll stick out like a peony in a bunch of snowdrops. There are rumours going around that she lives with our bearded Macheath, but nobody seems to know how true they are. The couple avoid each other at rehearsals, so the story is probably right.'

'Does Mrs Blaine still attend rehearsals?'

'No. I think Denbigh choked her off.'

'And our friend William Caxton?'

'Funny you should mention him. I've just had a letter from him.' Laura picked up an opened letter from beside her plate and handed it over. Dame Beatrice perused it.

'I see he asks whether it would be in order for him to attend the final rehearsal and take photographs,' she said. 'It would have been better to ask permission of Dr Denbigh, I should have thought.'

'I shan't bother to answer the letter. If he decides to turn up on Monday evening I can leave Denbigh to deal with him. Incidentally, he's to appear on stage at each performance to boost the pageant. It takes place the week after *The Beggar's Opera*. As for Caxton and the photographs he's after, the press will be there, anyway. Denbigh won't allow cameras at the actual performances, so one more person clicking away at the dress rehearsal won't make that much difference.'

'I see, too, that he requests the pleasure of a few words in private with you.'

'They'll have to be precious few. I'm on and off most of the time in the first Act and after that I'm prompting. Incidentally, you'll enjoy the scenes between Polly Peachum and Lucy Lockit. Sybil Gartner and Melanie Cardew so loathe each other that their passages of arms on the stage are almost too realistic.'

' "I shall now soon be even with the hypocritical strumpet",' quoted Dame Beatrice. 'I trust that the bottle of ratsbane is large and is well and truly labelled.'

'It is, and it's just as well that the stage directions call for Polly to drop her doped glass. I wouldn't put it past Melanie to add something toxic to the beverage if there was half a chance of Sybil's drinking it.'

'What fun you must have at your rehearsals. Do you think I might present myself at this one? If so, we could have George to drive my car and you would not need to drive home alone if the rehearsal does indeed last into the small hours.'

'Smashing idea,' said Laura. 'I'd like you to see the rehearsal. We're going to set the stage as well as put on the costumes and make-up. Our sets are rather fabulous. Our painters and carpenters have had the run of the college workshops as well as a lot of help from the students. We don't even end the play at the condemned hold. We're going to put Macheath on the hangman's cart and it's from there that he gets reprieved.'

'Realism indeed!'

'There's another bone of contention between Sybil and Melanie, I ought to tell you,' said Laura. 'I really thought Sybil was going to spit – literally, I mean. My own costume, as I'm Polly's mother and therefore very much a matron, is black and white. Polly was supposed to be dressed in a rather deep pink and Lucy in apple green, but when they tried the things on, Melanie, whose sallowness not even make-up can really disguise, looked so *awful* in apple green that she told Denbigh she really *must* have the pink dress plus a gypsy make-up put on really thick. Denbigh and the wardrobe mistress agreed, so it's going to be an apple-green Polly and a deep pink Lucy. Sybil was so furious that we half-thought she'd throw up her part.'

'But Dr Denbigh talked her round, I suppose.'

'Yes. He can be the soul of tact when he likes. I contributed my quota, too, when Sybil backed me into a corner to unload her grievances. Denbigh pointed out that the success of the show depended entirely upon her. *I* pointed out that *she* looks pretty in any colour, but that poor old Melanie needed all the help she could get to look even presentable on the stage. Between Denbigh and me we got Sybil soothed, but it wasn't easy. I just hope, with my fingers crossed, that Sybil won't rat on me and tell Melanie what I said.'

'I wonder whether Dr Denbigh has followed Sir Nigel Playfair and given *How now, Madam Flirt* to two of the ladies of the town, or whether he has put it in its rightful place in the script?'

'Oh, the latter. He's given it, as written in the text, to Polly and Lucy. It's one of their best efforts and I'm sure that, if Denbigh's production called for them to scratch each other's eyes out, they'd go to it with a will.'

'I am looking forward to this rehearsal. I wonder what Caxton has to say to you?'

'Not knowing, can't tell. Perhaps he wants to con me into trying to persuade you to let him do some more printing. He was awfully pleased to get that order for the tickets and posters. I expect he can do with a few commissions of that sort. It's a pretty poor sort of place in which he lives.'

'He may prefer it to a more palatial residence.'

'I don't know so much. He has a lean and hungry look which goes to my motherly heart.'

'Such men are dangerous,' said Dame Beatrice. 'Do not allow him to lure you into conspiracies.'

'Conspiracies?'

'Not the word I really mean.' She eyed her comely secretary with humour. 'Exchange the queen of fairies for the Green Man,' she said, 'and then repeat after me: "I am sae fair and fu' o' flesh, I'm fear'd 'twill be myself." '

'Good Lord!' said Laura blankly. 'Whatever would Gavin say?'

PART FOUR
Demolition

CHAPTER 16

It's a wise rabbit that stays in its own burrow.

The Saturday pre-dress rehearsal went as Laura had expected. It lasted until twelve-thirty on Sunday morning and was, in her words, a shambles. Nothing but the utter fatigue and ragged tempers of the players caused Denbigh to abandon it even at that hour. Then, to the cheers of the students, he said that he expected everybody to be back promptly at six-thirty on Monday evening. The rest of the cast groaned.

'Well,' said Laura, having, in the car on the way back to the Stone House, voiced her opinion of the company's efforts, 'if it goes anything like that on the night, people will be fighting round the box office demanding their money back. As for that wretched hangman's cart which the students are so proud of, if you ask me it's going to be far more nuisance than it's worth and anyway it isn't in the text. The opera ends in the condemned hold.'

'I thought the piece of apparatus was very effective. As for Mr Crashaw with the noose around his neck, he seemed to me a right and proper candidate for the gallows. I recognised him, of course, in spite of the beard,' said Dame Beatrice.

'Recognised him? You mean he really is. . . ?'

'Yes, indeed. You were absent, if you remember, when he called on me two or three years ago, so you did not see him when he was known as Thaddeus E. Lawrence, but you did tell me of the man who is down in the programme as Rodney Crashaw. That, in my opinion, settles it.'

'Why? – apart from your recognising him, I mean.'

'Come, come! Is this the student who harassed her junior

English lecturer with enquiries regarding the minor early seventeenth-century poets?'

'Richard Crashaw, 1613 (perhaps) to 1649? *R. Crashaw*! So you *do* mean it's Lawrence up to his old game of changing his name!'

'Well, one cannot blame him for not wishing to go down to posterity as a jail-bird.'

'Then our sumptuous blonde could be as we thought.'

'If you mean the young woman who was greeted on stage as Molly Brazen, yes, that is the first Mrs Lawrence whom I met in Blackpool as Coralie St Malo.'

'So, that's settled, too, is it? Very interesting. Well, it seems that she and Lawrence, *alias* Crashaw, have teamed up again. I wonder why?'

'It gives one furiously to think, does it not?'

'It gives *me* a headache. Do you think they spotted you at the rehearsal?'

'I have little doubt of that, but what of it? The truth is obvious.'

'Coralie murdered the second Mrs Lawrence and Lawrence buried the body. Consequently they now have to keep the tabs on each other. That would account for their getting together again.'

'This perspicacity is uncanny!'

'But if they know you've seen them not only together but so obviously part of the same set-up, aren't they going to ask themselves a few questions?'

'Again, I say, what of it?' The car slowed down to turn into the gateway of the drive up to the Stone House as she added, ' "He whom the gods love dies young." I used to think that this referred only to one's numerical age. I know better now, so let us cast care aside and repair to our beds "weary and content and undishonoured" .'

The car pulled up outside the front door and George saw his passengers out.

'We shan't need the car in the morning, George,' said his employer, 'so have your full quota of sleep. I am sorry to have kept you up so late.' She and Laura passed on into the house where they were greeted by a clucking Celestine in her dressing-gown.

'Henri has placed sandwiches and some wine in the dining-room, madame, and I am to make coffee.'

'No, no,' said Dame Beatrice peremptorily, for Celestine was known to be obstinate. 'You go to bed. As for Mrs Gavin and myself, we shall probably make a night of it.'

Celestine made disapproving Gallic noises and took herself off to join her slumbering spouse. Dame Beatrice and Laura went into the dining-room, where Dame Beatrice took one sandwich and a glass of sherry and Laura drank whisky and wolfed the rest of the provender.

'One thing,' she said, 'I suppose you're right and that, after all this time, nobody, least of all Lawrence and Coralie, is going to rake up the past.'

'I have an uneasy feeling,' said her employer, 'that the past is going to rake itself up.'

'What makes you say that? *I'm* the one who gets these premonitions, not you – and I'm very often, although not always, wrong.'

'This is not merely a premonition. I am uneasy on account of William Caxton.'

'Good heavens, why?'

'You told me that he came to one of the rehearsals with Mrs Blaine.'

'What of it? – as you would say. It was like her cheek to turn up, considering that she's done everything she can to sabotage our show.'

'Do you remember that, some time ago, I queried the name William Caxton?'

'Yes, but you gave me best over that, when I pointed out that it could be a common enough name.'

'The murdered Mrs Lawrence had a brother named Bill.'

Laura, a sandwich poised halfway to her mouth, lowered it and stared wide-eyed at her employer.

'You aren't suggesting – ?' she said.

'Mrs Lawrence's maiden name was Caret,' Dame Beatrice pointed out.

'A bit unusual, perhaps, but that's all.'

'Unusual, perhaps, as a surname, but not unusual in the printing trade.'

'In the printing – ? Oh, that little upside down V or Y which means something has been left out and is to be inserted? You don't suppose Caxton is proposing to insert a dagger into Lawrence, do you?'

'I suppose, going on the evidence of his not infrequent visits to his sister, that Mr Caret was fond of her, and you and I, I recollect, once had a conversation on the relationship between brothers and sisters.'

'But you think Coralie, not Lawrence, committed the murder. Lawrence only tried to cover it up by burying the body. That's your theory, isn't it?'

'We once mentioned Macbeth. There is no doubt – there was none in the troubled mind of Lady Macbeth – that both husband and wife shared guilt over the murder of King Duncan. In the case under review, just as Duncan's death was carried out at the instigation of the woman, but by the hand of the man, so the murder of Mrs Lawrence could have been at the instigation of the man, but carried out by the woman.'

'Well, she's strong enough, as we've said before, but you thought, after you'd met her in Blackpool, that she was one of these large, bonhomous women.'

'Henry the Eighth, by all accounts, was a large, bonhomous man. It did not prevent him from turning into a monster when monstrous behaviour suited his purpose.'

'And Coralie's purpose?'

'As I believe we have said before, after Sir Anthony's death Lawrence had become a very wealthy man. I still think Lawrence wanted his wife out of the way because she knew – or he *thought* she knew – something about that death which, if it were told to the police, might incriminate him, and I think that Coralie wanted her out of the way. . .'

'To clear a path to a re-marriage with Lawrence?'

'If, indeed, they were ever divorced. We have only Coralie's word that they were.'

'No wonder, if Lawrence spotted Caxton at that rehearsal to

which Clarice brought him, our Macheath refused to shave off his beard for the performances! I must sleep on this. You offer food for thought, dear Mrs Croc.'

Dame Beatrice did not attend the dress rehearsal proper. It went off so well that Denbigh was delighted, Laura filled with forebodings and the cast jubilant and self-congratulatory. There was only one hitch and that was merely temporary. The dressing-rooms at the town hall were at floor-level, not stage level. To reach the stage and its wings, therefore, the actors had to mount a short flight of stairs from the back of the O.P. side and pass the back-drop if their entrance was on the Prompt side.

Before the ingenious erection of carpentry and cardboard which represented the hangman's cart had been put together, therefore, the width of these stairs had been carefully measured and a wooden ramp made so that the contraption, mounted on perambulator wheels, could be pushed up on to the stage without damage to its flimsy sides. The perambulator wheels were disguised by curtains of hessian on which large, tumbril-like wheels had been painted by the indefatiguable students, and the cart had no back to it, as only its front elevation would be seen from the auditorium. The 'cart' was kept off the stage until what should have been the last scene in the opera as John Gay wrote it.

In Denbigh's production, between this last scene and the preceding one in which, confronted by four more of his wives – 'Four women more, Captain, with a child apiece' – Macheath announces that he is prepared to be executed – 'Here, tell the Sheriff's officers I am ready' – the curtain was to come down and to rise again to show Macheath standing on the fatal cart with his arms pinioned, a white cap over his face and head and the rope (a loop without a running noose) already around his neck. At the announcement of the reprieve, white cap and noose were to be whipped off and his arms ceremoniously freed, although there actually would be no knots to untie, as that might hold up the action.

All this had been carefully rehearsed, but, as it was not quite finished, without the cart until the pre-dress rehearsal. As the reprieve marked the end of the opera except for the last song and dance, the final scene came so late in the evening, when the cast were almost blasphemous with exhaustion, that it had been run through 'just for the sake of the motions' as Laura put it, and the cart left on the stage, from which the stage-hands removed it during the College dinner-hour on the morning of the dress rehearsal proper. However, when the time came to get it on stage again for the dress rehearsal, there occurred an unseemly and maddening hitch, the more annoying in that, apart from it, the rehearsal went well.

'Hey!' said one of the volunteer stage-hands, a student who had helped to construct the cart. 'Some funny ass has taken the wheels off! How are we going to trundle it on to the stage?'

'Manhandle it, I suppose,' said his friends.

'Not on your life. No room at the sides of those stairs. We'd break it. Except for the actual platform where the bloke stands, the thing's only made of cardboard, hessian and papier-mâché. Slip the word to the players. The chap will just have to stand at the right spot on the stage and imagine he's on the cart.'

'The noose won't reach his neck and I don't think we've got a longer piece of rope.'

'He'll have to do without a noose, then, won't he? After all, this is only a rehearsal. We must make sure it's all right on Thursday, though.'

'He won't mind about the cart. He's always jibbed a bit at that rope round his neck. Think he'd got a guilty conscience or something, wouldn't you?'

'Well, let him know. I'll have a scout round and see what's been done with those wheels. I'd like to lay hands on the blighter who perpetrated the merry jest, that's all.'

After the rehearsal Denbigh took the matter philosophically.

'If we don't find the wheels – and we're certainly not going to turn the back of the stage and the dressing-rooms upside-down tonight,' he said, 'we've got Tuesday and Wednesday to find some more wheels and for you chaps to fix them on. If the worst comes to the worst, I can tip off the cast to go back to the original script and have the reprieve from the condemned hold instead of from the gallows. It isn't, to my mind, such good theatre, but at least we should be carrying out the author's intentions, and that, I suppose, is something.'

On the following morning he telephoned the town hall and was answered by the porter on duty. He requested that the missing wheels should be traced if the porter could spare the time. As Denbigh had conducted public concerts in the town hall on previous occasions and was known to be moderately generous with his *pourboires*, the porter promised to do his best and to ring the College if the missing wheels came to light. They did, and were found on the electricians' gallery.

'One of your students having a bit of a game, eh, sir?' asked the town hall porter.

'Possibly. Well, now you've found them, you might put the wheels in the principal dressing-room and lock the door, would you? The students who will call at about half-past one to put the wheels on again will show you my visiting-card. That will prove their *bona fides*. All right?'

'Very good, sir.'

'And perhaps you'll just keep an eye on the cart when the students have re-affixed the wheels?'

'I'll do that, sir. In fact, I'll do better than that, sir. If that prop – we call 'em props, sir, these gadgets and things as are needed on stage, sir – if that prop, when the wheels is on, will go up that ramp what covers the steps on to the stage, sir, that prop will go in my cubby 'ole. Suppose I was to wheel it in there when the young gents have put the wheels on it again, sir – it's no height, so it won't catch the top of my door – and lock the door on it when I ain't in there, sir? How would that be?'

'That would be excellent, but what if you go off duty?'

'There'll be somebody here with a key, sir. If it isn't me, it will be my mate. I'll give him the tip-off as nobody ain't to touch that prop without they can perdooce your card.'

'Fine. I'll leave the whole thing in your hands, then, and, of course, I'll see you – er –'

'Thank you very much, sir.'

'Funny thing about that hangman's cart,' said Laura to Sybil and Melanie, with whom she shared a dressing-room. 'Who would play a daft trick like taking the wheels off it?'

'One of those beetle-brained students, of course,' said Melanie. 'Thought it funny, I suppose. All boys of that age have a warped sense of humour. Personally, I'm glad there are wedges under those wheels as an extra precaution. The stage slopes forward quite a lot. It would scare me silly if I was blindfolded and that cart began to move.'

'I never could abide Blind Man's Buff myself,' said Sybil. 'You feel so *helpless* when you can't see.'

'But he *can* see,' said Laura. 'I tried the hood on to find out what it was like, and I could see through it quite easily. It's only made of thin guaze. Anyway, thank goodness we don't have to be made up just yet.'

Laura's make-up took some time; Sybil's was simpler; Melanie was not to be made up until the beginning of Act Two, when, during the interval, Laura would have removed her own make-up, or most of it, and changed out of Mrs Peachum's costume in order to take over the prompter's stool and Sybil would have her face expertly touched-up, ready for her next appearance. Melanie, therefore, was supposed to be alone in the dressing-room, or wherever else she chose to be, for the whole of the first Act.

This was because she had rebelled against assuming the office of prompter for that Act, asserting, with vehemence, that the versatile Laura could prompt, whether she was on or off the stage and that she herself was prone to catch cold if she sat in a draught. As there was no doubt, as had been pointed out when the choice of a play was under discussion, that the wings of the town hall stage were definitely – some said fiendishly – draughty, Denbigh had given the job to Hamilton Haynings who, like Sybil, did not come on until Act Two and was well upholstered in Lockit's heavy costume.

Hamilton, whatever his private feelings about this particular chore, performed it faithfully for two nights, but on the Saturday evening nobody prompted at all, and as it became important, later on, to establish where everybody was and what he or she was doing at the beginning of the last scene of the play on the third and last night of the performance, these were Denbigh's arrangements for all three nights of the show.

The Player and the Beggar, that is to say one of the students and Ernest Farrow, would be on stage in front of the curtain. Behind the curtain would be Macheath, in the person of Rodney Crashaw (alias Thaddeus E. Lawrence) already mounted on the hangman's cart. Waiting in the wings would be the highwayman's gang, mostly students but also including two members of the society, Geoffrey Channing and Robert Eames, who had the parts of Ben Budge and Matt o' the Mint. On the other side of the stage and also waiting in the wings, would be Polly and Lucy (Sybil Gartner and Melanie Cardew), Filch (Mrs Blaine's son Tom), the drawer (from the inn scene), the turnkey and the second jailer (Lockit's assistants) and also the ladies of the town who included the blonde wardrobe mistress and Stella Walker, she who combined the parts of Jenny Diver and Diana Trapes. She had decided to revert to the costume of the former when she took her curtain calls, as she thought it far more attractive than that of the disposer of stolen property. The rest of the 'ladies' were students who had appeared also in the third Act as the women prisoners in Newgate gaol. These, having had their trial referred to the next sessions, were to celebrate this temporary reprieve with a dance, an activity in which the men students had declined to take part.

Behind all this rabble would be Peachum, in the person of James Hunty, and Laura, as Mrs Peachum, both waiting merely for curtain calls and both loitering in a short corridor on the O.P. side to be out of the draught which whistled on to the stage from the wings. Up to the end of the previous scene Laura would have been acting as prompter except on the third and last night, when she had announced her intention of abandoning this office after changing out of her stage costume, but retaining Mrs Peachum's rather startling make-up so that she could change back again quickly for the curtain calls. Until then she was to join Dame Beatrice, where a seat had been kept for her in the auditorium.

Provided that no prompting had been required during the performances on the Thursday and Friday, Denbigh had agreed to this arrangement, and it was not until the Beggar and the Player were actually on stage in front of the curtain that she needed to slip away to get back into the Mrs Peachum costume and join

James Hunty in the corridor. She expected to find Hamilton Haynings with him and, as the 'rabble' erupted on to the stage to perform the last dance before the final curtain, Laura supposed – rightly, as it turned out – that the three of them would retreat a little further into the confines of the sheltering corridor to be out of the way of the exits through which the rabble would pour when the curtain came down on the last Act.

Denbigh's original arrangement had been that the hangman's cart should be only just in view on stage to leave room for the dance when the reprieve should have been called and Macheath, in the words of the Beggar, 'be brought back to his wives in triumph'.

Crashaw, however, would have none of this arrangement. He insisted upon having the cart trundled to the centre-back of the stage. From here, before he was reprieved, he was to make the speech which belonged somewhat earlier in the Act. The duet between Polly and Lucy, 'Would I might be hang'd – and I would so, too! – to be hang'd with you – my dear, with you', was to precede this speech instead of coming after it – another slight alteration to the text.

'Like his damned conceit!' growled Hamilton Haynings when, at the unsuccessful pre-dress rehearsal, this innovation was actually staged. Hamilton had never quite got over his resentful disappointment at having been passed over for the principal rôle, any more than Marigold Tench had ceased to regret her precipitate action in walking herself out of a part when the opera was first under consideration. Marigold had attended every rehearsal (which, as a fully paid-up member of the society and its one-time leading lady, she had every right to do) in the sick hope that one of the three principal women players would either fall down on the part or give it up, but this had not happened.

She spent the actual performances behind the scenes acting as unsolicited dresser and assistant wardrobe mistress. Nobody wanted or needed Marigold's ministrations, but all accepted them in good part, sensing the frustration and disappointment which lay behind the seemingly kind actions.

The point of all this was that, as Laura pointed out later to Dame Beatrice, when the thing actually happened Marigold had been in as good a position as anybody else to overhear what Denbigh had said about the position of the hangman's cart on the stage.

'Apart from leaving more space for the last dance,' he had said, 'there's the safety aspect. I had not realised until Saturday –' (groans from the company which underlined their feelings about the long-drawn-out nightmare of that fiasco) '– I had not remembered that there is a rake on the stage down towards the footlights. By having the cart (it's on wheels, remember!) sideways on and almost pushed into the wings, however, the rake of the stage will hardly matter. If anything *did* go wrong, the wheels would only run the cart slantingly towards the prompt side, where there are plenty of people waiting in the wings.'

'Oh, rot!' said Melanie, looking adoringly at Crashaw. 'What *can* go wrong? He is the chief character! It would be absurd for him to make his last speech from the side of the stage and almost stuck out in the wings. He *must* be centre-stage. Stick those wedges under the wheels. That should fix them.'

Denbigh reluctantly gave in, only adjuring the students who were to act as stage-hands to make sure that the cart, as soon as it had been trundled up the ramp on to the stage, was securely anchored and the front wheels firmly wedged so that they could not revolve.

There was one other uncommitted person besides Marigold Tench who, at some point in the proceedings, was to be present. This was Mrs Blaine's William Caxton. She had insisted that at each performance he was to be brought to the front of the stage by Denbigh and introduced to the audience in one of the intervals as the leader and chief protagonist in the Caxton procession which was to take place in the following week. As there were to be street collections, all the proceeds of which would be devoted to charity, Denbigh could hardly refuse to do as she wished.

CHAPTER 17

Broke violence, madness, fear

In most amateur productions the first night is one of nerves and misgivings.

'Do I look all right?'

'I can't remember my first lines!'

'Will the press be here?'

'Oh, doesn't *anyone* know what's happened to the box of safety pins?'

'Who's pinched my Number Six?'

'Suppose they don't laugh?'

'I bet somebody's brought some ghastly infant who'll howl the place down in my first solo.'

'How's the house filling up?'

'Sybil isn't here yet. We're not really covered by understudies, you know.'

'I wouldn't put it past Ma Blaine to bring in a bunch of her Guild and bust up the show. They're all Women's Libbers, that lot.'

'Laura, you *will* give me a clear prompt if I dry up, won't you?'

The second night is apt to find the entire cast, even the principals, feeling slightly flat, but the third and last night sees everybody keyed up to the highest pitch, chattering, excited, confident, peeping from behind the curtain to watch the audience coming in, trying to find out how many bouquets will be presented and to whom they will go (although the second and third leads among the ladies are apt to make certain that each will receive at least one bouquet because she will have ordered and paid for it herself) and altogether the atmosphere will be noisily electric. The whole cast, assured of the success of the show, will love everybody with almost excessive fervour and the actors will even praise one another's performances, hoping, of course, for reciprocity on the lines of 'I'll scratch your back if you'll scratch mine'.

No doubt all this would have been the case on the third and final night of the Chardle and District dramatic, operatic and literary society's production of *The Beggar's Opera*, but for the presence behind the scenes of a *diabolus* or *diabola ex machina*. It became, later on, the self-imposed task of Dame Beatrice to expose this cuckoo in the nest.

However, it was not until the end, or almost the end, of the last Act that the Beggar's original thought was transformed into drastic and unrehearsed action and, as the poet says, 'violence, madness, fear' broke out and the opera ended in confusion.

With no suspicion, in spite of Dame Beatrice's dire prediction that the past was in process of raking itself up, that anything more untoward than, without a prompter, somebody in the last Act was going to dry up, or that the stage manager (the meek, devoted, hardworking Ernest Farrow who, as the Beggar, had only a few lines at the beginning and end of the piece) might mislay the bottle of ratsbane or some other important prop, Laura drove herself in her own small car to the town hall in good time to assume her costume and make-up, leaving Dame Beatrice to be piloted, a little later on, by George, for whom a seat had been booked in the front row of the balcony. From where he sat he had not only an excellent view of the stage, but of his employer in her seat near the O.P. end of the front row of the stalls. Next to her was to have been the empty seat which, at this last performance, would be occupied, after the first Act, by Laura.

As she entered the austere and stone-floored vestibule of the town hall, the first person Laura met was William Caxton wearing a lounge suit and a rather striking BBC style tie.

'Hullo,' she said, 'you're early. You don't go on stage to speak your little piece until the end of the first Act, do you?'

Denbigh, at first, had opposed the speaking of William Caxton's little piece from the town hall stage, claiming that it was entirely out of place in the middle of an early eighteenth-century comic opera, especially as the speech had been composed by Mrs Blaine herself in what she fondly believed was the English of Caxton's day. It ran as follows:

Hear me, ye merry gentles of good making,
And you, ye gentle ladies, with none quaking,
That here upon this stage I ye entreat
To think on them that looken well to eat.
When of your bonté ye do keepen kind,
Have Sister Charity, sweet maid, in mind,
And when Will Caxton's pageant ye endorse,
Give of your plenty that shall not fare worse.
For Edward Fourth, the Woodvilles and crook'd Dickon
Did favour Caxton and his books y-quicken.
I say you sooth, me needeth not to fain,
To give to charity shall be your gain.

The second to last line was pinched directly from Chaucer, whether Mrs B. knew it or not, but the rest of the lines were her own and she was proud of them.

As the money collected in the streets was to go towards the town council's Old People's Holiday Fund, Denbigh, as stated, had given in. He stipulated, however, that Caxton was to appear alone, thus placing an embargo not only on 'Edward Fourth, the Woodvilles and crook'd Dickon', but upon the Duke of Clarence (judicially killed before Caxton printed the second edition of the book on chess originally dedicated to him) and also upon that arch-economist, Henry Tudor. All of these were to have appeared on stage and in costume, and for each of them Clarice had composed what she called 'a little poem of gentle pleading for alms'. However, Denbigh had stood firm about all these 'extras'.

The first interval had been selected for Caxton's speech, this for more than one reason. For one thing, in Denbigh's production, the changing of the scenery from Peachum's house to the tavern near Newgate took longer than any other of the scenic changes for which the students had opted; for another, also, because the scene took some time to change, there was a more permissible break in the action at this point than at any other.

'Oh,' said Caxton, in reply to Laura, 'I'm to go on first tonight. Lord Denbigh's orders. He refuses to have a break in his show on the last night. I don't blame him.'

'Will you be in the audience after that?'

'No. I haven't a seat.'

'You can have mine for Act One, because I'm on, if that's any good. After that I shall want it for myself. I'm not prompting this evening. It's a good seat, front row, next to Dame Beatrice, but you'll have to hop out of it at the first interval because, as I say, it's earmarked for me and I want it.'

'Fair enough, and thanks awfully. So far, I've only been able to get a few glimpses of you from the wings. It will be nice to be out in front and have a proper view. The only trouble about your performance, you know, is that it must make the rest of the show fall rather flat.'

'You've got the offer of my *fauteuil*, so this tribute is unnecessary, although appreciated. Be seeing you.' She went to the dressing-room she shared with Sybil and Melanie and she thought no more about Caxton-Caret until the end of the first Act, when she slipped into the auditorium to claim her front-row stall.

'You were a riot,' he said, standing up as she approached. 'Many congratulations.'

'How did your speech go?' Laura asked.

'I received polite sporadic applause.'

'I believe, if you scouted round, you know, you could find an empty seat somewhere if you want to see the rest of the show.'

'Thanks. I might just do that. There's no bar here, so people don't seem to have moved about much.' He removed himself and Laura seated herself next to Dame Beatrice.

'There may not be a bar for the audience,' she said, 'but there's plenty of the right stuff flowing freely backstage. I could have topped myself up like a tanker at full load if I'd wanted to. Sybil is laying off, but Melanie, who's had the dressing-room all to herself until now, is what I should call in mellow mood and as I passed the door of the men's dressing-room it seemed to me that it was full of the joys of spring. I just hope the silly asses won't go and overdo it, that's all. There's quite enough last-performance *joie de vivre* about and around without adding any liquid sunshine.'

The second Act of *The Beggar's Opera* opens with dialogue. Macheath's gang reminisce and encourage one another. To them enters Macheath and later he is joined by the ladies of the town. Laura watched him closely, but decided that either, behind the scenes, discretion had proved the better part, or else that he carried his drinks well. The scene, which was lively and tuneful, went even better than on the previous nights. The dance met with spontaneous applause and there was a good deal of laughter at Sukey Tawdrey's speech: 'Indeed, madam, if I had not been a fool, I might have liv'd very handsomely with my last friend. But upon his missing five guineas, he turn'd me off. Now I never suspected he had counted them.'

After that, the business of Jenny Diver, Sukey Tawdrey, the pistols and the arrest of Macheath by Peachum and the constables brought the scene to a dramatic end, and the audience settled down to its boxes of rustling chocolates and its appreciative conversation while the scene was changed to Newgate gaol.

The first indication that there were to be certain departures from what had been rehearsed came with the entrance of Melanie as Lucy Lockit. There was no doubt that Melanie had not only looked upon the wine when it was red, but upon a fair measure of gin also.

She almost tripped over her own feet as she approached the perfidious Macheath, and her opening remark: 'You baish man, you!' was delivered with such concentrated venom that even Laura, accustomed as she was to Melanie's histrionics, was surprised and startled by the outburst and by the slurred sibilant, and when the next bit of the diatribe came out as: 'How can you look me in the faish after what hash parshed between ush?' surprise turned to certainty.

'My gosh!' said Laura in a whisper. 'The fool's as tight as a tick!' She left her seat, crouching low, and slipped round to the back of the stage. In the wings she found Ernest Farrow literally wringing his hands.

'What on earth are we to do?' he said. 'Melanie is drunk.'

'Superbly so,' agreed Laura. That this was no overstatement was proved a moment or so later. Upon the words: 'I could tear thy eyes out!' Melanie caught Lawrence a smack across the face which made him recoil and then she followed this up with a furious attack upon him which gave a vivid impression that she intended to carry out this threat.

Laura hissed at the students who were manipulating the curtain. As it came down, she and Ernest dashed on stage and pinioned the fermenting Lucy Lockit and hustled her into the wings, where she collapsed into a heap at the top of the O.P. stairs and broke into noisy, tipsy weeping.

Laura said to Ernest: 'I'll find Marigold Tench and tell her to get into my Mrs Peachum costume and stick some make-up on. You push out in front and tell the audience that Melanie has a temperature and can't continue. Crave their indulgence for a few minutes.'

At this moment Hamilton Haynings, who had been waiting on the Prompt side for his entrance as Lockit, Lucy's father, came across to them.

'What's happened?' he asked. 'Is she ill?'

'Yes. Get on and say so. All right, Ernest. You just put the word round backstage that we shall be resuming as soon as Marigold is ready.' She pulled the weeping Melanie to her feet. 'Come on. The dressing-room for you,' she said. There was a *chaise longue* in the dressing-room. There was also Marigold Tench. Laura pushed Melanie on to the former and tackled the latter.

'Put my costume on. We're much of a height,' she said. 'You know the book of words and the solos and duets as well as *she* does. This is the time for all good men to come to the aid of the party. I'll help you dress.'

'I feel sick,' moaned Melanie from the *chaise longue*.

'Then for pity's sake go and be it,' said Laura, hauling her up and dragging her towards the lavatory.

To the credit of the cast, nobody panicked or fluffed. The new Lucy proved more than adequate. She had had enough to drink to excite without intoxicating her and she put up what, under the circumstances, was a most meritorious perforamnce. The audience applauded her warmly, not only out of kindness to an understudy who had been called upon without warning, but as a tribute to a good perfòrmance.

As for Hamilton Haynings, he was seen that evening at his best. Going in front of the curtain in the lugubrious rusty black coat and breeches of the master gaoler, he had assumed the Friend and Champion of the People rôle which had served him so well in his public speeches before council elections. He was sorry, he said, for the hold-up. A doctor was in attendance upon Miss Cardew and had diagnosed a temperature of one hundred and three degrees. It had been very plucky of Miss Cardew to attempt to play the part when she was feeling so ill, (applause, for which he waited), but it was impossible for her to continue. He craved the indulgence of the audience for just a few minutes and bowed himself off to further applause.

The opera continued on its course. Having fulfilled the promise of Trinculo's foul bombard and shed her liquor, Melanie had fallen asleep on the *chaise longue*. The costume of Mrs Peachum proved to fit Marigold well enough, and Laura returned to her seat next to Dame Beatrice and was soon leading the applause for Lucy Lockit. She had been doubtful whether Marigold's *esprit de corps* would prove equal to the demands made upon it and was grateful that her doubts had been dispelled. Eventually a speech from Macheath, 'Tell the sheriff's officers I am ready', had brought the opera to the verge of its final scene.

Willing student hands trundled the fatal cart up the ramp and into position centre-back of the stage, but then came the second hold-up.

'Where are those wedges for the wheels?' demanded a voice.

'In the corner, top of the stairs, where we always put them,' came a reply.

'They aren't there now.'

'Well, ask the stage manager.'

But the wedges had disappeared.

'Look, the show must go on. We don't really need the wedges. They're only an extra precaution. The rope will hold the cart and two of you can stand by while Macheath mounts it. He's only up there a matter of minutes, anyway,' said Ernest Farrow, a speech which was remembered against him later. 'Do let's get the scene going. The chaps are ready in the corridor with the bouquets and we're running late already. Some of the audience have trains and buses to catch and the town hall staff expect to be off duty at ten-thirty.'

Backstage Macheath was proving recalcitrant.

'I don't want that beastly thing over my head and I don't want my hands tied,' he said.

'Of course you do,' said Ernest Farrow, hastening over to him. Two stalwart students, taking their cue from this, pinioned him, merely looping the cord over itself as they had done at the other performances. They crammed the white cap over his head and ears, and patted him on the back.

'Up you go, sir,' they said, hoisting him bodily on to the cart which, lacking the wedges for its wheels, wobbled a little but was immediately steadied by the students, one of whom arranged the loop around Lawrence's neck. It transpired, later, that he had not performed this simple act before, for the students who acted as stage-hands were changed each evening and depended upon the unlucky Ernest Farrow for their orders. He himself left them so that he could appear in front of the curtains where he was joined by the student who was acting as the Player.

Denbigh had cut this scene, as Laura knew, to a minimum. Each actor was to make two speeches only and then the curtain was to rise on Denbigh's *pièce de résistance*, Macheath on the hangman's cart and the 'rabble', hearing of the reprieve, rushing rejoicingly on to the stage – 'although, actually,' Denbigh had once confessed to Laura, 'I think they'd have been pretty shirty at being done out of the fun of a hanging.'

Before any of this could happen, Laura had gone backstage to wait in the corridor with James Hunty for the curtain-calls – there were to be three, at least, on this the last evening, more if the applause warranted them. The Beggar and the Player were already half-way through their short dialogue in which Macheath's reprieve was to be announced, but on this occasion the dialogue did not get finished in its original form, but sustained a surprising modern addition. It ended with these words:

Player	But, honest friend, I hope you don't intend that Macheath shall be really executed?
Beggar	Most certainly, sir. To make the piece perfect, I was for doing strict poetical justice. Macheath is to be hang'd; as for the other –

'Good God! Look out!' But he spoke too late. Something hit his companion from behind the curtain and, taken utterly by surprise, the unfortunate Player was precipitated into the orchestra pit where he found himself spreadeagled across the top of the harpsichord.

Behind the scenes there was immediate and utter confusion. The audience did not know whether to laugh at what some regarded as a rehearsed effect, or whether to view the Player's mishap with concern. Dame Beatrice, among the latter, darted forward to ask whether the Player was hurt. Reassured, she took the route she had seen Laura take and she and her secretary met face to face in the wings. Laura seized her employer's skinny arm and said:

'Quick! Lawrence! Do something! He'll hang himself!'

Together they hastened on stage.

CHAPTER 18

The anxiety of continual questioning

The inquest was fixed for the following Thursday, but before it could take place there was a police enquiry in which the whole cast, the stage-hands, the electricians and Dame Beatrice herself were involved.

'What caused you to go straight away behind the scenes, ma'am?'

'I was sitting in the front row of the auditorium and heard Mr Farrow, who was playing a part which took place in front of the curtain, exclaim: "Good God! Look out!" '

'What did you make of that?'

'I realised that a fairly heavy property, which was behind the curtain and was mounted on wheels, must have got loose. I could hear the sound of it as clearly as could the two actors.'

'What happened then?'

'One of the actors had his legs taken from under him by the force of the impact and was precipitated off the front of the stage. I am a qualified medical practitioner, so I went forward to see whether he was hurt.'

'But then you went backstage.'

'Yes. I realised that we had been witnessing an unrehearsed effect –'

'How did you know that?'

'I had been present at one of the rehearsals. I wanted to find out whether the actor who had been standing on the cart had suffered injury.'

'And he had, of course.'

'Yes, indeed. He was dead within moments of my arrival.'

'Further medical evidence indicates that he died of cerebral suboxia. Would you agree?'

'Certainly, although I think, in any case, he might have died of shock.'

'As the doctor first on the scene of the accident, you will be required to give evidence at the inquest.'

The next persons to be questioned were the two students who had been in charge of the cart.

'Did you not realise the possible danger of slipping a running noose over a pinioned and blindfolded man's head?'

'We only did what the stage manager had told us to do. We'd never done the job before. We didn't know it ought to have been just a loop and not a running noose. Somebody boobed, but it wasn't us.'

'You put the white hood over the actor's head, pinioned his arms behind his back and adjusted the rope around his neck. What else did you do?'

'We held on to the cart and helped him mount.'

'Why did you need to hold on?'

'Well, we didn't really think we needed to, because we'd been along to make sure the cart was securely fastened.'

'And was it?'

'Well, it seemed to be, but we weren't asked to test the fastenings. They *looked* all right.'

'So why did you hold on to the cart?'

'Well, rope gives a bit when you put any strain on it, and the cart wobbled a bit when he mounted it.'

'And after he had mounted it?'

'We left the stage, as we'd been told to do.'

'Where did you go?'

'Oh, well, over the road to get a quick one before the pub closed. When we came back to help with the clearing up, there was all this schemozzle – people talking, girls crying and the poor chap done for.'

That seemed to be all from the two students. The police then turned their attention to Ernest Farrow.

'Wasn't it a risky thing to entrust the safety precautions to two inexperienced students, Mr Farrow?'

'But I didn't!' exclaimed Ernest, too indignant at this suggestion to feel alarmed by the presence of police. 'I *never* liked that cart and the noose. The opera doesn't call for it and I've always been against any tampering with the text. Still, the producer wanted it that way, so, as stage manager, I was bound to carry out his orders.'

'So you really tested the safety measures yourself?'

'Certainly I did. The cord which anchored the cart was perfectly secure. The person to blame for this regrettable affair is the practical joker who hid our wedges and untied the cord which fastened the cart to the back of the stage. I only hope his conscience is giving him hell. All the same, I can't understand what could have happened. The wedges were only an extra precaution, after all. We had held more than one rehearsal without them, and the rake of the stage isn't enough to send the cart careering away like that.'

'Why, then, did you decide to use them?'

'One of the girls – the ladies – got nervous, so I had them made just to pacify her.'

'But at that last performance they were missing?'

'Yes. We couldn't hold up the opera looking for them, so we carried on, but I assure you, Detective-Superintendent, that the cart was perfectly safe when I left it. I secured it myself and inspected my fastenings just before I had to go on in front of the curtain for my last bit of dialogue.'

'The cord was knotted to secure it?'

'Certainly.'

'Are you an expert on knots, Mr Farrow?'

'I wouldn't claim that, but I was a Scout and knowing about knots was part of Scout training.'

'So what kind of knot did you use to secure the cart?'

'The same as I would use to secure a boat – a round turn and two half-hitches. You can't have anything much more secure than that.'

'What, in your opinion, then, caused this fastening to come undone and release the cart?'

'Human agency, as I said, Detective-Superintendent. A stupid, thoughtless, pinheaded practical joke by one of the students. I only wish Denbigh could find out which one.'

'We've inspected the stage, sir. As you say, it slants gently down towards the footlights. Is that usual?'

'Yes, I think so. It gives a better view of the people coming on-stage from near the back.'

'Is the stage at the College where, I understand, the earlier rehearsals took place, similarly tilted?'

'No. It's just a flat platform. It's not the College stage; just a big dais in the music room.'

'So a student might not have realised the danger at the town hall. Thank you, sir. I think that's all. Oh, one more thing.'

'Yes? I may tell you, Detective-Superintendent, that the thriller programmes put out by the BBC have familiarised me with that particular gambit.'

'Sir?'

'This business of pretending you've finished with a witness and then suddenly throwing a question at him, thinking him to have been disarmed.'

'Oh, dear me, sir, we don't work along those sort of lines, I assure you. Still, if you feel like that, I will save my question for another time.'

'No, no. Out with it, please. I am not a nervous man, but I dislike being left on tenter-hooks.'

'Very well, sir. You are an officer of your operatic society, I believe?'

'I'm the honorary treasurer, yes.'

'I notice that you are inclined to place the blame for what has occurred on the College, sir. I suppose you're quite sure none of your members might have had a spite against the gentleman?'

'Enough to murder him? Good heavens, no, of course nobody has!'

'I had no thought of murder in mind, sir, but, suppose the accident had not ended fatally, could it not have made this Mr Crashaw look rather ridiculous, with his cart running away from him and he left hanging on to the backdrop, or something of that sort?'

'The cast would know how dangerous that would be,' said Ernest, after a pause for thought. 'His hands weren't really tied, of course – the bonds were just looped over – but even so, taken by surprise, he might not have had time to release himself and clutch at the halter round his neck to save himself from strangulation. Oh, and that's another thing! That halter was never meant to have a slip-knot. Everybody in the cast knew that, and we are all mature, responsible people, all old enough to know better than to play stupid practical jokes such as changing a fixed loop into a running noose.'

'Even the schoolboy, Thomas Blaine, sir?'

'I assure you, my dear chap,' said Dr Philip Denbigh, 'that my students are not involved. I have instituted, in collaboration with the principal of the College, the senior staff and the head students, man and girl, the strictest and closest enquiries. You yourself have done the same. There is no student who was present at the performance who cannot be accounted for by witnesses. Apart from that, the students in question are third years. They have sat their final examinations and are intending to teach children. They all know better than to play dangerous practical jokes, I do assure you.'

'Mr Farrow tells me the same about his members. Your students are young and high-spirited, though, sir, wouldn't you agree?'

'Certainly they are, but they are not dangerous lunatics, Superintendent.'

'One or other of them took the wheels off that cart at the dress rehearsal, sir.'

'You have no proof of that.'

'And somebody hid those wedges which were supposed to be put under those same wheels on the last night of the performance. Even if somebody had accidentally or deliberately pushed against the cart, the wedges would have held it.'

'You must look elsewhere for your culprits. My students are not responsible for the tragedy which has occurred.

'Perhaps you can suggest who *is* responsible, then, sir.'

'What do you mean by that?'

'No offence, sir, but you, as producer of this opera which, I understand, has been in rehearsal for several weeks, must have had your finger on the pulse, so to speak. Were there any little rifts, for example, between the deceased and anybody else in the cast? Clashes of temperament, jealousies, quarrels?'

'Not so far as I am aware. Mr Crashaw was not my first choice for the part, but when I gave it to him there was little or no ill-feeling among the others.'

'What happened to your first choice, then, sir? Couldn't he fill the bill?'

'Oh, it was nothing like that. He was fooling about on a trampoline at his school – he's a teacher – fell off it awkwardly and was taken to hospital with a fractured leg. It was a very nasty crack, I believe, silly young ass!'

'So there's no suggestion he could have been present at the town hall on Saturday?'

'Ask the hospital!'

Young Tom Blaine came next on the list, but as it was clear, from Ernest Farrow's evidence, that the mischief with the fastenings of the cart must have been done not earlier than a few moments before Ernest's own last dialogue with the Player in front of the curtain, young Tom was able to alibi himself without difficulty.

'I was supposed to have a short scene with Lockit – that's Mr Haynings – in Act Three,' he said, 'but Dr Denbigh cut it out because it's a bit rude. It's about. . .'

'Never mind what it's about, lad. Where were you during the last scene, where, as I understand it, Mr Farrow and one of the students have a short dialogue in front of the curtain?'

'I was in the porters' room playing backgammon with Mr Caxton until my mother took him home, then I played with one of the porters. You can hear the applause from the porters' room, so that was my cue to get into the corridor with the other principals ready to take our curtains. The porters, both of them, came with me, because it was their job to hand the bouquets. They get pretty good tips, you see, for staying late and seeing to the bouquets.'

As both porters vouched for all this, there was no more to be said. Granted, however, that Lawrence's death was the result of a practical joke which had misfired, there was one aspect of it which dangled – almost literally – in the Superintendent's mind. This was the running noose, instead of a knotted loop, in the hangman's rope. He tackled Ernest Farrow again.

'When you tested your knots which anchored the cart, sir, did you also take a look at the noose?'

'No, I'm afraid I didn't. We left it in position from one night to the next, you see. It was fastened to one of the iron girders so that it dropped straight down, forming, as it were, a plumb-line from near the roof, the weight of its knot, where the noose was, holding it pretty steady, and all the stage-hands had to do was slip it over Macheath's head.'

'At what point in the proceedings would they do that, sir?'

'It was after they had pinioned and blindfolded him and helped him up on to the cart. They had a small step-ladder – one of those ladder-stool things which ladies use in the kitchen – to get up to reach the noose, and then they just put it lightly round his neck.'

'So he himself wouldn't have been aware that on that last evening it had a running noose instead of a knotted loop in it?'

'I suppose not,' said Ernest, unhappily. 'You know, Detective-Superintendent, I'm wondering whether, by some oversight – and don't think I don't blame myself, because I do – I'm wondering whether that slip-noose could have been there all the time.'

'All the time, sir?'

'Yes, for the dress rehearsal and all three performances. We didn't use the noose at the dress rehearsal, and the Thursday and Friday nights went off without a hitch, so it never occurred to me to check the noose. I'd checked it at the pre-dress rehearsal –'

'What exactly was that, sir?'

'You may well ask,' said Ernest, his voice rising in remembered anguish. 'You never saw such a *fiasco* in your life. We were at it until half-past twelve at night. My poor mother was convinced that I must have met with an accident until I phoned her at midnight and told her I'd be home as soon as I could.'

'But you inspected the noose on that occasion, sir?'

'Yes, I did. Not that we ever got around to that last scene on that occasion. We were all so tired and wretched that we didn't finish the opera.'

'At what point during that rehearsal did you inspect the apparatus, sir?'

'At the first interval. The porter at the town hall, under my directions, had climbed up and looped the rope over the girder and I myself had inspected the noose to make certain that it was perfectly safe. The other end of the rope was slung over the girder, not fastened in any way. If the cart had, for any reason, begun to move, the rope should have slid off the girder and fallen on to the stage, thus averting any possible danger to Macheath.'

'Yes,' said the police officer grimly, 'it should have slid off the girder, but it didn't, and the question is, if not, why not? I may as well tell you, sir, that I've climbed up to take a look at that rope myself. It's fastened securely. The porter must have mistaken your instructions if they were as you say. I'll see what he has to tell me.'

What the porter had to tell him was simple and conclusive.

'Yes,' he said. 'Mr Farrow wasn't too keen on climbing high ladders, so he give me his instructions about looping the rope over the girder. Myself, I didn't think it would hold, that girder being unpainted iron and of a circular nature; still, I done as I was told. Well, they has this rehearsal what looked like going on till all hours, so at ten-thirty I packs it in. Firstly I finds Councillor Haynings and puts it up to him as ten-thirty were closing time. He says the rehearsal is a right mess, so they couldn't give up yet, but as how I could go off dooty, him taking full responsibility.'

'So he locked up the town hall that night instead of you doing it?'

'Me leaving him my keys, which he returned personally on the Sunday morning, directly he come from church, to my own house. Well, I unlocks on the Monday morning, as usual, and has a look round and sees as the rope, as I knowed it would, had slid off the girder and was on the stage, so I phones up Councillor Haynings, me having his number because of him being chairman, and tells him. So he says, "Well, fix it, man, fix it." So I gets me ladder again and fixes it, that's all. I never done nothing wrong. Orders is orders, that's what I allus says.'

CHAPTER 19

We have drawn the curtain across an empty stage

'But you don't go along with the verdict at the inquest, do you?' said Laura.

'Death by Misadventure? It is an interesting choice of words,' said Dame Beatrice.

'Wouldn't Accidental Death have done as well? Not that I believe it, any more than you do.'

'In the present case, Accidental Death may be ruled out, I think. There were far too many coincidences for this to have been an accident, and the coroner's jury seem to have shown an intelligent grasp of the niceties of language in phrasing their verdict.'

'In other words, *they* suspected it was murder, and *we* know it was murder, but where's the proof?'

'I shall find it. I am not in favour of punishment – none of us should be authorised to punish any other of us. . .'

'All miserable sinners, you think?'

'Well, the casting of stones is, perhaps, a hazardous operation, for it is undeniable that we all live in glass houses.'

'So what?'

'Society, we are told, must be protected. Why, I hardly know.'

'Protected from Clarice Blaine?'

'Why Clarice Blaine?'

'Well, she was the only person who would have wanted to muck up our show.'

'With her son taking part in it? Have you no conception of a mother's love?'

'Well, I've two children of my own, but is that germane to the issue?'

'No, it is not, but if Clarice Blaine had decided to muck up our show, as you term it, why should she wait until the very end of the opera? The press had attended, had scribbled down their opinions and had left in order to get their copy into the local papers in time for next week's editions. The "mucking up" came too late to be effective. If I read Mrs Blaine aright, she is not a woman to waste her sweetness on the desert air.'

'Very true. Besides, although I wouldn't put much past her, I don't see her going as far as murder but, of course, to be fair, murder may have been the last thing anybody intended.'

'Let us look at the facts.'

'Well, the basic fact is that Lawrence was hanged.'

'It seems to me that the other facts are these: as we are certain that this unfortunate man *was* murdered . . .'

'You call him unfortunate? He got away with murdering poor old Sir Anthony.'

'There is not, and there never will be, any proof that he murdered Sir Anthony.'

'But look at what he gained by that old man's death! Anyway, what do you think happened on the last night of *The Beggar's Opera*?'

'Ah, there we are on less controversial ground.'

'I wouldn't agree. Everybody seems able to produce a watertight alibi. In fact, they can all alibi one another.'

'There is one possible exception, I think, but first let us look at those whom we might suspect of wanting Lawrence out of the way.'

'Hamilton Haynings, for one. He badly wanted to play Macheath. James Hunty did, too, but he's the easy-going type and Peachum is a pretty fat part, anyway. I can't think of anybody else and, besides, the argument about Mrs Blaine applies to everybody else in the cast. The time to have got Lawrence out of the way so that someone could pinch his part would have been at the dress rehearsal, not at the very end of the last performance.'

'There was a reason why the murder could not have been committed at the dress rehearsal. If you care to cast your mind back, I think you will see what that reason was.'

Laura wrinkled her nose in thought.

'I don't get it,' she said.

'Then, as the patient schoolmaster said to the ill-behaved boy, I fear we do not see you at your best.'

'Ah!' exclaimed Laura. 'The deed couldn't have been done at the dress rehearsal because the wheels were off the cart. Anyway, the rope which carried the noose should have slipped off the girder as soon as the cart began to move.'

'As it demonstrated when it slipped off the girder of its own accord after the pre-dress rehearsal was over. I wonder how many of the cast and, of course, the stage-hands, knew that the porter had secured the rope to the girder?'

'All the stage-hands were students. We can discount them. The point is that we come back again to Hamilton Haynings. We know he knew about the rope because he was the one who told the porter to fix it. On the other hand, he's ruled out, you think, because of the time the deed was done and, of course, unless there was some private difference between the two men of which we know nothing, the comparative weakness of the motive.'

'I am wondering whether the murder may have had nothing to do with the opera itself at all. You are going on the assumption that this was a man's crime. I think we might do well to take a look at some of the women in the cast.'

Laura looked troubled.

'If you're thinking of Melanie,' she said, 'I can assure you that once we'd dragged her off the stage she was too far gone to have climbed back on again. She smacked Crashaw's – Lawrence's – face and then, to all intents and purposes, was a spent force.'

'Yes,' said Dame Beatrice, 'and there's another thing. I looked at the tilt of the stage – the rake, do they not call it? It is obvious, but slight. Too slight, in any case, to account for the velocity with which that comparatively light vehicle careered towards the curtain.'

'Somebody gave it a pretty hefty shove, you think, and that couldn't have been Melanie for the reason given. There were plenty of people milling about behind the backdrop, though. There's a passage-way through from the O.P. to the Prompt side because there's only one flight of steps from the dressing-rooms on to the stage.'

'The dressing-rooms, yes,' said Dame Beatrice. 'How many were in use that night?'

'Four. Hamilton, James and Lawrence shared one; Melanie, Sybil and I had another, and Marigold was in and out of it most of the time when she wasn't in the wings. The other two were used by the chorus.'

'Miss Tench took over Miss Cardew's part.'

'When Melanie got too sozzled to go on, yes.'

'Well, I cannot allow matters to rest. The first person I want to see is the porter who secured the rope to the girder. Please put me in touch with Councillor Haynings. He will know which porter it was.'

'I wonder whether he has found those wedges? They would have saved the situation.'

'That is one of the things I shall speak to him about.'

An unhelpful bit of information, but one which cleared up a very minor mystery, came through on the telephone call to Hamilton Haynings. He gave the porter's name and then said, 'I've just had Denbigh on the 'phone. Two of his students – he's been grilling them mercilessly, he tells me, because of the seriousness we all attach to the disappearance of those wedges – two of the youngsters have confessed to removing the wheels from the cart. Wanted to put them on a contraption of their own so that they could take part in some fancy race on the College sports ground. Said they put them back in plenty of time for the Thursday performance and, of course, they did.'

'And the wedges?' asked Dame Beatrice.

'They swear they know nothing about the wedges and Denbigh believes them. He points out that to borrow the wheels put us only to temporary inconvenience – hardly that – but to take away and hide the wedges could have been dangerous, and it was. I blame Farrow. He was stage manager and should have provided substitutes for the wedges.'

'He would hardly have had time or opportunity for that. He appears to have relied upon the fact that the cart was secured to the back of the stage.'

'Yes, by a method which, although secure enough in itself, can be untied in a twinkling.'

'But not by accident, Mr Haynings.'

The porter's information was a little more helpful, but not much. On the morning of the dress rehearsal quite a number of the cast had turned up at the town hall for various reasons. Mr Farrow was there, fussing about and picking up bits and pieces *here* and putting them down *there* and then going back to what he'd first thought of; then there was Mrs Blaine. She had brought young Tom in the car because he had finished his school examinations and she wanted him to help her check something or other in the Council Members' room to which, of course, she had a key. There was also one of the ladies who spent about an hour sorting over the costumes which were all laid out or hung up in the dressing-rooms and two other ladies were helping her. Mrs Blaine popped on to the stage while he was up the ladder fixing the rope because she had heard somebody trying to play pop music on the harpsichord which, as it was only hired and did not belong to the College or the society, she thought ought to be stopped.

'No, there's no reason why any or all of 'em shouldn't have knowed I was up the ladder, ma'am, and as some on 'em must have seen the rope a-laying on the stage where it had dropped and, what is more, heard me 'phoning Councillor Haynings, my office door being open, the weather being warm and my room small, they could have knowed what I was a-doing of and why I was a-doing of it.'

The harpsichordist? He 'reckoned as it was the young chap as was with the fellow as was doing the lights'. He had already 'told 'em both off for misusing of the town hall electricity. Ought to have been at work, and was doing a mike on account they both still worked for Mr Haynings what had also employed 'em in the building trade afore he retired.'

'What does Miss Cardew do for a living?' Dame Beatrice asked. 'Do you happen to know?'

'Ah, I do. Got her own ladies' hairdresser's business in the high street. My missus and my daughter both goes there. She knows how to charge, too!'

'Do you want me to make a hair appointment for you?' asked Laura, as they left the town hall.

'That can wait, and may not be necessary. What do we know of Miss Marigold Tench?'

'Marigold? She's on the staff at Cyril Wincott's school. Teaches French, I believe. Shows off a bit by introducing French phrases into her conversation.'

'Can you contact the school by telephone?'

'Yes. They used not to be in the book so that parents and tradespeople couldn't waste the head's time by ringing up at inconvenient moments, but now that heads have secretaries to answer the 'phone, the schools are all in the yellow pages. What shall I say?'

'Are you sufficiently well acquainted with Miss Tench to invite her to tea?'

'After helping her cope with Melanie and the demon rum, I think I may be.'

In the words of Wodehouse, Marigold turned out to be 'an upstanding light-heavyweight.' She had a defiant chin, a compelling eye and a facility for speaking in the French tongue which apparently delighted Celestine who, with beaming face, introduced her into the drawing-room as 'Mademoiselle Souci Tanche'.

Dame Beatrice cackled greetings in French while Laura stood grinning. Mademoiselle Souci Tanche said that she had spotted that Celestine was a Frenchwoman and that she herself preserved the *entente cordiale* whenever possible.

'I suppose,' said Marigold, at a pause in the tea-time conversation, 'you've asked me here for some reason apart from *mes beaux yeux*.'

'Not to beat about the bush,' replied Laura, 'they *are* rather a secondary consideration at the moment.' She caught her employer's eye and Dame Beatrice took up the running.

'I remember you as Lucy Lockit, do I not? she said. 'A most enjoyable performance until its unfortunate ending.'

'I had to take on the part at a moment's notice, so I don't think I did too badly.'

'I would have supposed you to have rehearsed for weeks.'

'Thanks, but no. The girl who had the part – I expect Laura has told you – wasn't fit to go on.'

'Dear me!'

'Yes, got herself plastered. Personally, I don't think any man's worth it.'

'Any *man*?'

'Oh, yes. She was immersed enough to confide in me. She was expecting to marry that man who was strangled. Crashaw, you know. They'd had a pretty hectic affair, I gathered, and she confidently expected marriage to come of it before the baby arrived. Lucky for her, as it turned out, that she *did* get tight, or I might have thought that she'd done Crashaw a mischief. He'd just turned her down, you see. That's why she got sloshed and smacked his face. His was a very funny accident, though, if you ask me.'

'Did you leave Miss Cardew in the dressing-room when you went on stage?'

'Yes, fast asleep and with two of the students who had been in the "ladies of the town" scene to keep an eye on her. I didn't like the wild way she'd been talking before she *fait dormir*.'

'Threats?'

'Yes, to kill herself. She's the type to do it, too. I'll tell you one funny thing, though, which it's hard to believe, but is perfectly true: Crashaw has left her all his money.'

'How do *you* know?' asked Laura.

'Ma Blaine and I witnessed the will. It was quite short. He invited us to read it. He said,

"Melanie is going to have my kid. I've had two wives, but no kid. I can't do the obvious thing by her, so, if anything happens to me, this may do something to put me right with her."'

'Did Melanie herself know about the will?'

'She must have done. She was shouting the odds loudly enough about it just before she passed out under the influence. I should think half the cast must have heard her.'

'Including the wardrobe mistress?'

'*La bombe blonde*? Oh, yes, definitely. She was flitting about from dressing-room to dressing-room all the performance, putting in a stitch here and chasing up a shoe there and touching up somebody's make-up with a dab of powder. You know the kind of thing. The only part she herself had was that of one of the chorus ladies, you see, so most of her time she was off-stage.'

'And *I* see,' said Laura, when the bi-lingual guest had gone, 'what you meant when you said there was one person who couldn't be said to have an alibi. There was nobody who could vouch for the wardrobe mistress the whole of the time, and she could have heard what Melanie was shouting about the money.'

'I wonder what she had planned, if anything, before she heard Miss Cardew's drunken ravings? She must have known about the affair between Miss Cardew and Lawrence, since she herself lived with him. The knowledge that she could expect nothing at his death, except what an appeal to the courts might bring her, probably precipitated an act which, up to that point, could have petered out in mere wishful thinking. Melanie's baby and the loss of the money clinched matters, I think. Besides, Lawrence may have threatened to inform upon her for the murder of his wife. Well, I think we have enough to take to the police.'

'Do we want to avenge Lawrence's death? He was a rotten type, you know.'

'A tainted wether of the flock, meetest for death? Maybe so. I was thinking of *Mrs* Lawrence's death, not his. I feel sure that Coralie killed her.'

'We can't bring that murder up, can we?'

'No, but the police may. That case is not closed.'

'How about William Caxton? Of course we don't *know* he's Mrs Lawrence's brother, do we?'

'Yes, we do. He told me so when he occupied your seat during the first Act. I asked him whether William Caxton was a trade name and he agreed that it was and confessed to being Caret.'

'Well, he must have been the person that Lawrence went to prison for – to get away from, I mean. He must have threatened Lawrence in some way, and, as you've just pointed out, he *was* in the town hall that night.'

'I think young Tom Blaine's evidence absolves him. He was playing backgammon with Tom until Mrs Blaine collected him from the porters' room to run him home. He was not in the town hall when that cart received the push which hanged Lawrence.'

The police, having listened to Dame Beatrice, paid a surprise visit to Lawrence's house. They held a search warrant. The missing wedges were found at the bottom of Coralie's wardrobe. She did not attempt to explain how they had come to be there. She was formally charged with Lawrence's murder.

'He had it coming to him,' she said, 'the heel! I meant to have his money, but he double-crossed and done me out of it. Born crooked, I reckon. Well, I've been give bracelets in me time. on't I get a couple from you blokes?' She grinned amiably at e officer arresting her, patted her hair and went quietly.

MORE VINTAGE MURDER MYSTERIES

EDMUND CRISPIN

Buried for Pleasure
The Case of the Gilded Fly
Holy Disorders
Love Lies Bleeding
The Moving Toyshop
Swan Song

A. A. MILNE

The Red House Mystery

GLADYS MITCHELL

Speedy Death
The Mystery of a Butcher's Shop
The Longer Bodies
The Saltmarsh Murders
Death and the Opera
The Devil at Saxon Wall
Dead Men's Morris
Come Away, Death
St Peter's Finger
Brazen Tongue
Hangman's Curfew
When Last I Died
Laurels Are Poison
Here Comes a Chopper
Death and the Maiden
Tom Brown's Body
Groaning Spinney
The Devil's Elbow
The Echoing Strangers
Watson's Choice
The Twenty-Third Man
Spotted Hemlock
My Bones Will Keep
Three Quick and Five Dead
Dance to Your Daddy
A Hearse on May-Day
Late, Late in the Evening
Fault in the Structure
Nest of Vipers

MARGERY ALLINGHAM

Mystery Mile
Police at the Funeral
Sweet Danger
Flowers for the Judge
The Case of the Late Pig
The Fashion in Shrouds
Traitor's Purse
Coroner's Pidgin
More Work for the Undertaker
The Tiger in the Smoke
The Beckoning Lady
Hide My Eyes
The China Governess
The Mind Readers
Cargo of Eagles

E. F. BENSON

The Blotting Book
The Luck of the Vails

NICHOLAS BLAKE

A Question of Proof
Thou Shell of Death
There's Trouble Brewing
The Beast Must Die
The Smiler With the Knife
Malice in Wonderland
The Case of the Abominable Snowman
Minute for Murder
Head of a Traveller
The Dreadful Hollow
The Whisper in the Gloom
End of Chapter
The Widow's Cruise
The Worm of Death
The Sad Variety
The Morning After Death